W9-BEB-942

Mary Anne and Camp BSC

**Other books by
Ann M. Martin**

Rachel Parker, Kindergarten Show-off
Eleven Kids, One Summer
Ma and Pa Dracula
Yours Turly, Shirley
Ten Kids, No Pets
Slam Book
Just a Summer Romance
Missing Since Monday
With You and Without You
Me and Katie (the Pest)
Stage Fright
Inside Out
Bummer Summer

BABY-SITTERS LITTLE SISTER series
THE BABY-SITTERS CLUB mysteries
THE BABY-SITTERS CLUB series

Mary Anne and Camp BSC
Ann M. Martin

AN
APPLE
PAPERBACK

SCHOLASTIC INC.
New York Toronto London Auckland Sydney

Cover art by Hodges Soileau

If you purchased this book without a cover, you should be aware that this book is stolen property. It was reported as "unsold and destroyed" to the publisher, and neither the author nor the publisher has received any payment for this "stripped book."

No part of this publication may be reproduced in whole or in part, or stored in a retrieval system, or transmitted in any form or by any means, electronic, mechanical, photocopying, recording, or otherwise, without written permission of the publisher. For information regarding permission, write to Scholastic Inc., 555 Broadway, New York, NY 10012.

ISBN 0-590-48227-0

Copyright © 1995 by Ann M. Martin. All rights reserved. Published by Scholastic Inc. APPLE PAPERBACKS and THE BABY-SITTERS CLUB are registered trademarks of Scholastic Inc.

12 11 10 9 8 7 6 5 4 3 2   5 6 7 8 9/9 0/0

Printed in the U.S.A.   40

First Scholastic printing, June 1995

The author gratefully acknowledges
Nola Thacker
for her help in
preparing this manuscript.

CHAPTER 1

Pike's Peak.

The two words just jumped into my head as I watched Mallory Pike's seven younger siblings and Pow Barrett Pike, the Pikes' basset hound, playing a game of freeze tag.

Pike's Peak is this famous mountain out west that was a sort of landmark for the European settlers who were headed for the coast.

But the Pike's Peak I was thinking about is written this way: Pikes' Peak.

Because the Pikes were at the peak of their energy and activity. Okay, it's a pretty dumb pun, but peak is an almost *quiet* way of describing what I was watching. Adam, Byron, and Jordan, who are ten and are identical triplets (although they weren't dressed alike — they'd die these days before they'd dress alike, except maybe for a practical joke), were charging around making wild grabs at everybody. Vanessa, who is a budding poet, was dodging madly and shrieking, *"Freeze, freeze, if you please!"* Nicky, who is eight, and Margo, who is seven, had hunched themselves into horrible, contorted, frozen shapes. Claire, who is five, was laughing and jumping out of the way as everyone pretended they were about to grab her and then "missed." And Pow was racing in and out among them all howling "Hoo, hoo, hoo!," his big, long ears flapping as he ran.

Mallory, who is eleven and a junior member of the Baby-sitters Club (of which I am the secretary, but more about that later) as well as the senior sibling of the Pike family, nudged me with her shoulder. "You're it," she said with a grin.

I grinned back. We were sitting on the back steps of their house. What were we doing? You guessed it. Baby-sitting. Pike-sitting. The Pikes always ask for two sitters when they call the Baby-sitters Club. Not that the Pikes are bad kids or hard to handle or anything like that. But there *are* a lot of them and they have tons of energy (see above).

Claire made a grab at Jordan, who toppled over. "I'm frozen, I'm frozen," he wailed and writhed on the ground before "freezing" into a pretzel shape.

"You iced Jordan, Claire," said Adam. "But you won't ice me!"

"Baroo! BarooOOOO!" howled Pow ecstatically.

Mal rolled her eyes. "I think all this spring and school-about-to-be-out stuff has gone to the triplets' heads."

"I know," I said. "It's just too bad we can't channel some of that energy and use it for, I don't know, electricity or something."

"Yeah. Dawn would approve of that. It would be very environmentally correct." Mal was talking about Dawn Schafer, who is my stepsister, one of my two best friends, and a fellow member of the BSC. She is also, in case you hadn't guessed, very environmentally conscious. But more about that later.

I laughed. "I wonder how you'd do it?"

"Beats me," Mal said. We sat in comfortable silence for awhile and watched the frozen victims all come back to life and start over again.

Then Mal said, "I can't believe school will be over in just three weeks!"

"Me either. And I can't wait. I feel like all I've been doing lately is studying for tests and doing homework and baby-sitting. I haven't even had time to clean up my room lately."

"Don't worry. Your room will still be there."

"I know. But it bugs me. I like to have things neat."

Mal grinned. "In my family, I just like

3

knowing where things are. With eight kids and two adults picking things up and putting them away, watch out!"

"Hey, when you've got a stepmother like Sharon putting things away, watch out!"

We laughed. Sharon Schafer Spier, who is my stepmother and Dawn's mother, is, well, an *imaginative* housekeeper. I've found cans of beans on bookshelves and books in the linen closet. Sharon is absentminded that way, just the opposite of my father, the king of neat. But opposites attract, they say. And my father and Sharon are crazy about each other. I'm pretty crazy about Sharon, too. It's nice having her for a stepmother, and extra nice having Dawn as one of my two best friends *and* my sister . . .

Wait a minute. I'm getting ahead of myself. I'm Mary Anne Spier. I'm thirteen years old. I'm kind of short, and I have brown hair and brown eyes. People say I'm sensitive and that's probably true. Sometimes it's a pain, because the littlest, dumbest things can make me cry (even some commercials on television). And I'm shy, too. On the other hand, I think being sensitive and shy helps me listen to people and be more understanding.

I live in Stoneybrook, Connecticut, where I'm in eighth grade at Stoneybrook Middle School. I've lived here all my life, most of the time as an only child and a half orphan.

Half-orphan sounds sad, I guess. But my mother died when I was just a baby, so I can't really remember her. My father raised me by himself.

My father was strict, but loving. He was, as I got older, a little overprotective. He was so worried about being a single parent that I guess he was overcompensating. Anyway, for a long time, he made me wear my hair in braids and chose all these really little kid clothes for me. But with the help of my friends, I was finally able to bring him around. I can buy any kind of clothes I want now (within reason) and I even got a new haircut not too long ago. I also got a kitten named Tigger.

There's Logan, too. Logan is the cutest boy in all of SMS and possibly Stoneybrook. He looks just like Cam Geary, the star (okay, so I'm not that objective, but still, it's true). He's from Kentucky originally and has this cool southern accent.

And he's my boyfriend. See how much my father's changed?

But that's not the biggest change in my father's life — or mine, for that matter. The biggest change is Sharon.

That's right. Dawn's mom.

You see, Sharon grew up in Stoneybrook.

5

In fact, years ago she used to date my father. But they lost touch after high school and Sharon ended up in California. Then when Dawn's mom and dad got divorced, Sharon moved back to her hometown with her two children, Dawn, and Dawn's younger brother, Jeff.

That's where we come in. Dawn and I had already become best friends (in fact, I'm the one who suggested that Dawn join the BSC, which is what we call the Baby-sitters Club). Then we discovered the ancient romance between my dad and her mom. So, with a little help from us, the two of them started dating. And fell in love all over again.

And got married.

Which proves that opposites do attract, as I said before. My dad, Mr. Neat and Organized, is a lawyer. He alphabetizes the books on his bookshelves. He arranges his socks by colors in the drawer. He's never, ever late for anything. His car looks as if he just bought it.

You get the picture.

And Sharon? Well, I've found a letter that she meant to mail stuck in the bathroom cabinet, and dishwashing soap in the laundry room. Plus Sharon, like Dawn and Jeff, is pretty health-food conscious. Sharon and Dawn never, *ever* eat red meat (Jeff does sometimes, I think) and they avoid sugar as if it were poison. My dad is a mashed potatoes and meat loaf kind of guy.

But all of that didn't matter and still doesn't, I guess, because they love each other. So now we're a blended, bicoastal family. We're blended because we're two smaller families that have become one big family. And we're bicoastal because Jeff eventually decided to move back to California with his dad (and Dawn just recently spent much too long a time out there on a visit).

We live in this neat house out on Burnt Hill Road. It's an old farmhouse built back in the seventeen hundreds and it even has a secret passage that might be haunted.

Although I'd always wanted a sister, my new family was a bit overwhelming at first (for Dawn, too, I found out). But we really care about each other. I like living in a big family. Well, compared to the Pikes it's not such a huge family, but you see what I mean. I wouldn't have it any other way.

"Huge," said Mal.

"Huh?" I said, wondering if she'd turned into a kind of mind reader.

"The chunk of time after school is out at the end of June."

"What do you mean?" I asked.

"Well, the camps that most of the kids go to don't begin for three whole weeks. And the civic center won't start its summer activities until the middle of July."

I was beginning to see what Mal was talking about. "Three weeks of kids out of school, parents still at work — and lots of jobs for the BSC," I said.

"Maybe too many," said Mal. "Since we're, you know, a little short-handed."

I nodded. Neither Mal nor I particularly wanted to talk about it. We were short-handed because one of the members of the club had quit not too long before. Stacey McGill, our treasurer, had just left the BSC — and her friends — for her boyfriend and his group of "more sophisticated" friends.

It was true. They were more sophisticated than most of us in a way. But it still hurt.

Quickly I said, "So what're we going to do about it? Get a new member of the BSC?"

"We could, I guess," Mal said. "But who? And where?"

We were quiet for a moment, thinking it over. At last we looked at each other and shook our heads.

"I vote we make this club business," Mal said. "Bring it up at the next meeting."

"Good idea," I said.

"Come play!" Claire shrieked.

"Okay." Mal suddenly grinned. She jumped up.

"Hey," I said. "Wait for me!"

We played freeze tag until Mal's mother came home.

Maybe I wasn't all that sophisticated. And maybe, I thought, making a dive for Mal, I didn't care if I ever was.

We often eat dinner a little later than most people, because my father works late. He was almost too late for dinner that night. We were just sitting down at the table when we heard the back door open.

"I'm home and a happy man!" he announced, pausing in the doorway of the dining room. He leaned over to give Sharon a quick kiss. "Just let me hang up my coat and put my briefcase . . ."

His voice trailed off as he hurried down the hall.

He was back in a minute. "Hmmm. Smells good. What's the entree?"

"Three-cheese macaroni," said Dawn. "It's a recipe I made up."

"Sounds great," said Dad. He sat down. He smoothed his napkin onto his lap. He picked up his fork.

We'd all started eating by then. It was a great dinner, California-vegetarian-Schafer style, with some Spier touches thrown in, such as the double garlic and onion toast I'd made.

I put chopped up little chunks of garlic and onion on top of the toast and it looked pretty good.

I waited for my dad to taste everything and talk about how delicious it was—something he almost always does.

But he just sat there, holding his fork, looking around the table.

I knew something was up.

I put down my fork. Was something wrong? But my dad looked pretty cheerful. And hadn't he just announced that he was a happy man?

So now two of us were holding our forks and not eating. Dad met my eyes and he grinned. He cleared his throat.

At almost exactly the same time, Sharon and Dawn looked up. Sharon put her fork down, too. Dawn stopped in mid-macaroni bite.

"Richard?" said Sharon. "What is it?"

My father cleared his throat again. "Yes. Well. I have some good news. Some *outstanding* news. Some excellent news."

"Richard!"

"Our law firm is merging with another firm — "

Sharon immediately looked relieved. "Oh, yes. I remember you'd talked about that being in the works."

"Yes. It's all set. It's a great opportunity for

us." My father was using his "lawyer" tone of voice now. I had to smile.

"Congratulations, Dad," I said.

"Super, Richard," said Dawn.

"Thank you, both of you." My father looked pleased. "I'll be traveling more, at least at first." He cleared his throat for a third time. "Beginning with a two-week trip to Cincinnati in July."

"Two weeks!" Sharon smiled at Dad. "Sounds important."

"It is," Dad said.

Sharon looked at Dawn and me. "Well, we can 'bach' it," she said. She pronounced it "batch."

Dawn and I gave her puzzled looks, but my dad let out a shout of laughter. "I haven't heard that term in a long, long time," he said. "I think my grandfather used it."

" 'Bach' it?" asked Dawn.

"Make like bachelors. Be bachelor girls," explained Sharon.

It sounded pretty old-fashioned to me.

"Cool," Dawn said. "We'll order take-out food *every* night and stay up late and . . ."

I was beginning to get the picture. "And have wild parties!" I added.

Dad and Sharon looked at each other. I could see them making all kinds of "eye conversation," if you know what I mean.

"Sounds good to me," Dad said at last. He looked down at his plate as if he'd just discovered it was there. "Dinner!" he said. "I'm hungry!"

We all started laughing then.

CHAPTER 2

"This meeting of the Baby-sitters Club will come to order," Kristy Thomas said.

"Who ordered the sour cream potato chips?" asked Claudia Kishi from the back of her closet.

"Me," said Mal, who was sprawled across Claudia's bed.

"Me, too," said Jessica Ramsey, aka Jessi, who was sitting on the floor next to the bed.

"Ahem," said Kristy, clearing her throat. I gave her a startled look. For a moment, she'd sounded just like my father.

"Here," said Claudia, backing out of the closet. "Now where are those jujubes?"

We started laughing, because Kristy, who was the one frowning at Claudia for not paying attention now that the meeting had come to order, was holding the jujubes.

"Okay, okay," said Kristy good-naturedly.

"Dues," said Dawn and we groaned. We

13

always do. It's practically a requirement — along with paying the dues! The dues cover BSC expenses and the occasional pizza blast.

It was Monday (and dues day), and it was 5:31, and we were in Claudia Kishi's room. The BSC meets three days a week, Mondays, Wednesdays, and Fridays, from five-thirty to six. That's when our clients call us to set up appointments. That's also when we take care of club business.

There are eight of us in all: me, Mallory, Claudia, Kristy, Jessi, Dawn, Shannon Kilbourne, and Logan. We weren't all there, though. Logan is an associate member and doesn't come to many meetings. (He does help us out, though, when we can't fit a job into our schedules or have too many jobs to handle.)

Kristy is the president of the BSC. That's not only because she's the world's most organized person (more organized than my father, even) but also because the BSC was her brilliant idea.

It happened this way: one day Kristy was listening to her mother call baby-sitter after baby-sitter without success. That's when it hit her. What if a person could call just one phone number and reach several experienced sitters?

That's how the Baby-sitters Club got started. At first it was just four of us: Kristy, me, Claudia, and Claudia's new friend Stacey McGill, but the idea caught on and we soon had to expand. Now, even with eight of us, there's plenty of work. And plenty of room for Kristy's organizational talents. Today the BSC, tomorrow the world.

Kristy was my first best friend. We lived next door to each other on Bradford Court. (Claudia lived across the street from us, in the house where she still lives). Kristy and I are very, *very* different. Not outwardly, so much. Kristy is short, even shorter than I am, and she's a pretty casual dresser. She wears what we call her uniform: jeans, a turtleneck or T-shirt, and running shoes. She often wears a cap with a picture of a collie on it, in memory of her family's old dog Louie, who was a collie. He died not too long ago.

Having a "uniform" is one way of being organized, I think. I mean, Kristy doesn't have to spend any time worrying about what she's going to wear.

Anyway, Kristy has brown eyes, like me, and brown hair (although hers is longer), and she lives in a blended (but not bicoastal) family, too. And we're both pretty stubborn, in our own ways. Some of the fights we had as kids were monuments to stubbornness!

But that's where the similarities end. Because I'm quiet and shy and Kristy is very sure

15

of herself and not afraid of making her opinions known. In fact, some people have even said she has a big mouth.

Part of the reason Kristy is so outspoken, I believe, is because she grew up with two older brothers and one younger brother. Her older brothers tease Kristy pretty often. But it doesn't bother her. She just teases them back and goes on.

Kristy's father left when Kristy was a kid. She still remembers him, but he never gets in touch with her, except maybe to send a Christmas card or a birthday card (late). He has a new family now, in California. Kristy never talks about him.

After Mr. Thomas left, the Thomases had a really tough time. David Michael was still a baby, Mrs. Thomas was working hard to make ends meet, and Kristy and her brothers, Sam and Charlie, had to help out and work hard, too.

Then things changed. Oh, Kristy's mom still works hard. But they don't live on Bradford Court anymore. They live in a real, live mansion. That's because Kristy's mom met Watson Brewer (who is a real, live millionaire) and they fell in love and got married.

Now Kristy's family includes not only her three brothers and her mom, but Watson and his two children by a previous marriage, Karen and Andrew, plus Emily Michelle, who is Vietnamese and was adopted by Kristy's mom and stepfather. There's also Nannie, who is Kristy's maternal grandmother, who came to help look after Emily Michelle, plus assorted pets, and maybe even a resident ghost!

You have to be organized *and* outspoken in a situation like that. So it's not surprising that Kristy is always thinking and always coming up with great ideas. Some of them backfire, but that never stops Kristy. That's probably one of the reasons the BSC is so successful.

Other big reasons? Us, of course. The other BSC members.

Claudia Kishi is our vice-president. She was one of the first members of the BSC and she is the only member who has her own phone line. That's why we hold the meetings in her room. Clients can call, and we don't have to worry about tying up the phone line so the rest of her family can't use it.

Claudia is totally cool. She wants to be an artist. She has had her own private art show and has even won a prize for her work. She sees art potential in everything, even stuff most of us would call junk — such as junk food. Claudia loves junk food and she always keeps a good supply of it stashed around her room, along with the Nancy Drew books she likes to read, and of which her parents also disapprove. So it's hardly surprising that she's used junk food as the inspiration for some of her artwork.

Actually, Claudia herself is a work of art in progress (that's what she would say). She makes most of her own jewelry and she's always trying on outrageous combinations of clothes and colors that shouldn't look good together. On Claudia, though, the clothes and the colors work.

But although Claudia is very creative and one of the best-looking girls in the school, with her long black hair and her perfect skin and her dark brown eyes, she is not so cool when it comes to traditional schoolwork. This is ironic, because Claudia's sister Janine is a real, live genius, who takes college courses, although she's only in high school. But Claudia would rather be almost any place except in school. She thinks creatively, and that doesn't always lead to good grades in, well, less creative subjects such as math and spelling.

Still, although English and spelling are Claudia's least favorite subjects, she once joined the staff of the school newspaper, the SMS *Express*. She wrote a column called "Claudia's Personals," which she started when she was looking for the perfect boy.

You've already met Dawn, sort of. Dawn started in the BSC as our alternate officer. Her job was to fill in when one of the other officers couldn't do her job, which is what Shannon does now. However, Dawn's taken over as the treasurer since Stacey left. (Or maybe Stacey was fired. At the last meeting of the BSC that she attended, everybody said some pretty awful things. It ended with Stacey saying she quit and Kristy saying Stacey couldn't quit, she was fired. Stacey and Claudia were best friends and they still talk to each other, but mostly we don't mention Stacey. It's very sad.)

But anyway, Dawn is a good treasurer even if she's not the math whiz of the world like Stacey. She has her own, casual, easy-going style and is as striking as Claudia. Like Claudia's, Dawn's hair is long, but it is pale, pale blonde, almost white, in fact. She has light blue eyes and pale skin and gets freckles if she stays out in the sun too long.

But freckles aren't enough to stop Dawn from loving the beach. She misses her brother and father — and the California sunshine and the California beaches. She's even a member of another baby-sitting organization when she's in California, one that she helped start because the BSC is such a great idea and because Dawn missed it. It's called the We ♥ Kids Club.

Dawn is practically a vegetarian. She's very environmentally conscious. She brings her lunch to school in brown paper bags (which she uses over and over again) and never wraps her sandwiches in plastic wrap. And while we consume mass quantities of junk food at Claudia's, Dawn usually munches on an apple.

In spite of her intense feelings about the environment, Dawn is very laid-back and practical. In fact, it's still a surprise to me that she loves ghost stories so much. And believes in ghosts. Maybe it's part of her willingness to accept people as they are, even ghosts.

Shannon Kilbourne, who is acting as our alternate officer now, is the only member of the BSC who goes to private school — Stoneybrook Day School. Shannon is very serious about school. She's a member of a couple of clubs, is an honor student, and takes French.

Shannon lives across the street from Kristy. She has thick, curly blonde hair, high, high cheekbones and blue eyes. She has a Bernese mountain dog named Astrid, who just had puppies. Astrid had puppies once before, and Shannon gave one of them to Kristy's family after Louie died. That's how Shannon and Kristy became friends. In fact, David Michael named the new puppy after Shannon.

Shannon is sometimes quiet, but she is very sure of herself in her own way, just like Kristy, and very organized in a Kristy-like way, too. Because she is so involved in school, she

20

doesn't have time to take as many baby-sitting jobs as the rest of us, but with summer coming, Shannon said she was looking forward to earning some extra money. "Except," she told us, making a face, "they've given us a summer reading list, too."

We all went "euuuw," but we also knew that Shannon would read every single book on the list.

Two other BSC members who are best friends are Mal and Jessi. Mal and Jessi are junior officers. As sixth-graders, they aren't allowed to baby-sit at night unless they're taking care of their own siblings, so they take a lot of afternoon jobs.

Jessi wants to be a ballet dancer and takes special dance lessons every week. She's even danced in a real ballet, a performance of *Swan Lake*. Jessi is slender with brown eyes and brown skin and carries herself like a ballet dancer. She wears her black hair pulled back in a ballet dancer's bun. She is very disciplined and gets up every morning *before* her alarm goes off at 5:30 so she can practice ballet at the barre that her family built in the basement for her.

Like Mal, Jessi is the oldest kid in her family, but she has only two younger siblings — her eight-year-old sister, Becca, and her baby brother, Squirt. And like Mal, Jessi *loves* horse stories, especially horse stories by Marguerite Henry.

Mal loves horse stories, too. In fact, she'd like to be a children's book writer and illustrator some day, and I wouldn't be surprised if she writes about horses. Meanwhile, she works as hard at her writing as Jessi does on her ballet or Claudia does on her art. Mal has red hair and pale skin with freckles, and to her eternal despair wears glasses and braces. She's also secretary of her class at school. She used to be one of our baby-sitting charges, but she's a little too old for that now. And when we realized how good she was at baby-sitting and how much experience she'd had (with all her brothers and sisters), it seemed only natural to invite her to join the BSC.

Logan Bruno (who wasn't at this meeting) is, as you know, an associate member of the BSC. You should also know that he's a good baseball and football player, likes track, and is a good baby-sitter. He's average height, with blue eyes and blondish brown hair. He's got a great sense of humor and he can be very romantic. He can be a good friend, too. Logan is also stubborn and sometimes bossy, which is why we broke up for awhile. But we worked things out and I'm glad we did.

Finally, there's me. I'm the secretary of the

BSC, which means I'm in charge of the record book. I keep track of our jobs, and who is available when our clients call to ask for a baby-sitter. And so far, I've never, ever made a mistake.

In addition to the record book, we have a club notebook. In fact, as Kristy was answering the phone and taking down the information about a baby-sitting job, Mal was writing in the notebook.

The notebook was also a Kristy idea. We write up our baby-sitting jobs in it: details about new clients, information about who is having trouble at school, who's developed a dislike for this food or that activity, who might be afraid of ghost stories but love horse stories, what happened at various jobs. It's very helpful and means we are extra-prepared when we baby-sit. And it is important for a baby-sitter to be prepared.

We had a lull in the phone calls. Mal finished writing in the notebook. Claudia took a jujube, put it between two potato chips, and gulped it down.

I met Mal's eye. "Okay, everybody," I said. "We've got a potential problem."

Kristy lifted her head like a bull who's seen a red flag. "What're you talking about? Is one of the kids we sit for having trouble?"

"Nope," I said. "The problem is summer."

"Summer is *never* a problem," said Claudia flatly.

Dawn grinned. "I agree. The beaches are warm, school is out, what could be better?"

"Business is going to be better," said Mal. "Think about it." Then she explained about camp and the community center and the three-week lag between those activities and the end of school. "Unless we take on more baby-sitters," she concluded, "we may have more work than we can handle."

"Wow, you're right, Mal." Kristy looked thoughtful.

"Who else can we get to work with us?" Shannon asked. No one mentioned Stacey. Conspicuously.

The silence built up. Claudia muttered something, then shook her head.

"I could ask some friends at my school if they could help out, but . . ." Shannon's voice trailed off.

And then Kristy's face lit up. "Camp," she said.

We waited.

"Camp," said Kristy again. "Camp BSC. A baby-sitting camp! A day camp! Like the mini-camp you and Dawn once had, Mary Anne." It was perfect. We knew immediately that it would take care of the problem. If all eight of the current members of the BSC, including Logan and Shannon, were counselors, the camp could probably handle about twenty kids. And our clients would be very, very happy.

"Perfect," I said aloud.

"Super perfect," said Claudia.

The phone rang again. And again. We were kept very busy the rest of the meeting setting up baby-sitting jobs.

It looked as though the summer rush had already begun. We'd thought of the idea of Camp BSC just in the nick of time.

CHAPTER 3

We were gathered in Claudia's room for the Wednesday meeting. Logan had joined us. Kristy hadn't exactly told everyone it was an emergency meeting, but I had a feeling she'd presented the need for everyone's attendance in pretty urgent terms.

"Tomorrow?" Dawn nodded solemnly at the phone. "I'll check and get right back to you. . . . Yes. . . . Thank you." She hung up the phone and looked at us. "Mrs. Papadakis needs someone tomorrow afternoon."

I flipped open the record book and ran my finger down the list. "Jessi, it's the one day you don't have ballet practice. Do you want to use your free afternoon on a baby-sitting job?"

"No problem," said Jessi. "Hannie and Linny and Sari are great kids. Sign me up."

I did, while Dawn called Mrs. Papadakis back.

The phone stopped ringing for a moment and Logan stopped throwing popcorn up in the air and trying to catch it in his mouth to ask, "Okay, so what's the deal here?"

Kristy said, "The deal is summer . . . but I'll let Mary Anne and Mal explain."

"You have some complaints about summer?" Logan pretended to be shocked. I hadn't told him about Camp BSC. I wanted him to come to the meeting with an open mind.

Mal grinned and pushed her glasses up her nose. "Summer's great, Logan. Unless you're a parent with kids who've just gotten out of school and it's too soon for camp or the community center to have started."

"Oh . . ." Logan thought about that for awhile.

Shannon was quick to get to the point, as usual. She said with her characteristic briskness, "And this is where the BSC comes in."

"Right!" I said. "We save the day. We fill up the free time . . ."

"We sleep late," said Claudia plaintively.

We all cracked up. Kristy picked up a piece of popcorn and flicked it at Claudia. "Later, Claud. Later in the summer we sleep late."

I hid a smile at that. It was hard to imagine Kristy *or* Shannon sleeping late. Dawn could manage it, I knew from past experience. I

27

didn't mind sleeping late myself, although not as a rule. (Also I have this gray kitten who thinks that if he's up at daylight, his owner should be, too. Tigger and I have had many, many discussions about this. I have lost most of them.)

Logan loved to sleep. He claimed that hot weather and sleep went together naturally. But I knew that nothing would keep him away from a baseball game or a pick-up game of basketball or football.

Mal?

She answered the question just then by saying, "Sleep late? The Pike family motto is 'Get up *now*.' "

And of course, we all knew that Jessi was up at 5:29, every single day, summer or winter, to practice at the barre.

"What's the plan, then?" asked Logan.

Mal and I exchanged glances. I said, "Go for it, Kristy."

Kristy took a deep breath. "Camp BSC," she said. "A day camp for our clients. We can hold it at Dawn and Mary Anne's. We've done stuff like that there before. Their yard is big. And on rainy days we can move into the barn."

"Outstanding idea," said Logan.

Shannon nodded. "I like it."

Dawn leaned forward. "Mary Anne and I

talked to Richard and Mom and they've agreed. But since they both work, they want us to have at least one adult nearby on call. We thought Mrs. Prezzioso and Mrs. Braddock might agree to it, since they live nearby and since they are home during the day."

"Good thinking," said Kristy. "Let's call them."

I flipped through our record book and read their phone numbers out and Kristy made the phone calls. Both Mrs. Braddock and Mrs. Prezzioso not only said yes, but they thought it was a terrific idea, and Mrs. Braddock signed Matt and Haley Braddock up "full-time" on the spot.

After that, everything just seemed to fall into place. We agreed that camp would run from nine A.M. to five-thirty P.M. so parents could drop their kids off on the way to work and pick them up afterward. We also decided kids (and their parents) could choose a half-day or a full-day program.

"Let's see, we'll need supplies, the usual camp supplies," said Kristy.

Claudia said, "Art supplies: paint, paper, crayons, glue, glitter, clay . . ."

"Games, sports stuff," said Logan immediately, beginning a list of his own.

"Whoa, whoa, whoa!" said Dawn. "We'll make a list. Then we'll estimate how much everything we want is going to cost and see how that stacks up next to how much money we have in the treasury."

"How much money *do* we have?" asked Kristy.

"We're doing pretty well," Dawn said. "But we can't buy everything."

"Refreshments," said Claud. "Snacks for morning and afternoon. The kids should bring their own lunches, but we can have fruit juice and milk for them to drink."

"We can buy some of that stuff as we need it. After the parents pay the fees for our camp, we can buy refreshments out of the fees," Shannon pointed out.

Mal said, "The important thing is having everything set up so it goes smoothly the first day. If the kids have fun the first day, then if something goes wrong after that, they are less likely to notice."

"First impressions are important," Kristy said seriously.

My hand was flying across the page as I wrote. We kept firing ideas around the room, stopping only when the phone rang. Claudia agreed to make fliers that we could give or mail to our clients as soon as possible. We discussed field trips and activities and menus.

And then Kristy said, "Circus! Circuses!"

As you know by now, Kristy is full of ideas.

So when she leaps into the middle of a conversation with these random words and sentences, we don't automatically assume she's crazy. Instead we wait. Because we suspect that she's having one of her Ideas.

She was. "A circus," Kristy explained. "That should be the theme of Camp BSC. It can be part of the activities, see? Making costumes, athletic activities, decorations, props . . . and then at the end of the camp we can give a circus."

"Excellent!" exclaimed Claudia. She'd loved circuses when she was little and once had had a circus birthday party. It hadn't turned out quite the way she'd expected, but clearly it hadn't made her dislike circuses.

"Lions and tigers and bears, oh my," Shannon quoted from the movie *The Wizard of Oz*.

"Karen and her friends went to a circus camp once. That's where I got the idea." Kristy said modestly. Karen is her younger stepsister, Karen Brewer. "They loved it, so they should love this, too."

The phone rang one last time. Kristy took the call and we scheduled one more appointment.

Then Kristy looked at her watch. "This meeting of the BSC is officially adjourned," she said.

But we didn't leave right away. Claudia

said, "Can we have candy apples? I *love* candy apples. Are they hard to make?"

Dawn said, "Candy apples? Do you know what that does to your teeth?" But she was smiling.

"Cotton candy," said Mal dreamily. "Even with braces, I know I could handle cotton candy."

"I want to be a ringmaster," Kristy said. She grinned good-naturedly when we all started laughing.

Just then there was a knock on the door.

"Hey, come on in," Claudia said.

It was her sister Janine. "I believe you should know that Kristy's brother is here."

"Ohmigosh!" Kristy leaped to her feet. "Thanks, Janine. The meeting really *is* adjourned."

"Wait for me!" Shannon said. She was getting a ride home with Kristy.

Kristy and Shannon raced out the door. The rest of us followed a little more slowly. I confess, I was feeling pretty excited about Camp BSC.

And I knew, with the club involved, it was going to be one super circus camp. Lions, tigers, bears, and all.

CHAPTER 4

School was out. Just like that. And I hardly noticed it. I mean, I was glad that taking tests and having to get up at the same time every morning and all of that was officially over for the summer.

But with Camp BSC starting the following Monday, I was almost too busy to take it in.

Ever since our brainstorming session, we'd been working pretty hard getting everything organized. Twenty-two children had signed up for the camp. They were Kristy's stepbrother Andrew Brewer, Alicia Gianelli, and Jamie Newton, all four years old. The oldest were Vanessa Pike, Haley Braddock, and Linny Papadakis, who are nine. In between were Mal's sibs Nicky, Margo, and Claire; Kristy's stepsister Karen Brewer, and her best friends Hannie Papadakis and Nancy Dawes (all seven); the twins Marilyn and Carolyn Arnold (eight); Matt Braddock (seven); Jessi's sister Becca; Charlotte Johanssen (eight); Kristy's brother David Michael (seven); Bobby Gianelli (seven); Ricky Torres (seven); Natalie Springer (seven); and Chris Lamar (seven).

Whew.

More about our BSC campers: Ten of our campers attend Stoneybrook Elementary School: the Pikes, the Arnolds, Haley, Becca, Charlotte, and David Michael. Eight of them attend Stoneybrook Academy: Karen, the Papadakises, Nancy, Bobby, Ricky, Natalie, and Chris. And eight of them had gone to a circus camp before! Karen, the Papadakises, Nancy, Ricky, Natalie, Chris, and Bobby (who'd gone to a different circus camp from the other seven).

So maybe a circus camp wasn't a *totally* original idea, but we all loved it, especially Claudia. She kept calling our barn the "Big Top" and suggesting that I train Tigger for the "Lions and Tigers Act."

But goofing aside, Claudia had designed these super tie-dye shirts for us to wear. We hadn't told the kids about the circus idea yet, though. We decided to wait until they'd settled in the first day and then announce it.

By Sunday night, we'd done all we could do. The only big question remaining was the weather. Would it rain?

It didn't. I woke up extra early and opened

34

my eyes and started smiling immediately. No matter what else happened during the day, the sun was shining. It was a sign, I decided, that Camp BSC was going to be a success.

Dad and Sharon left, wishing us luck, and Claudia arrived with a last minute load of art supplies, which she hustled out to the assortment of tables we'd set up by the barn. We'd lined the tables with cups filled with colored pencils and crayons and paper for everyone to draw on. That was going to be the first activity of the morning for the kids, until everybody had arrived and settled in. We'd even decided to have a theme for the kids to draw. Today, the first day, we'd suggested that they draw their favorite circus animal.

Logan showed up next on his bicycle (he looks *very* handsome on a bicycle), followed by Mal and Jessi, along with four more Pikes and one more Ramsey.

Dawn, who'd been hovering by the front door with me, gave Logan a friendly punch on the shoulder, Kristy-style, and said, "I think I'll go check out those circus animals." She grinned at me, gave me an exaggerated wink, and then grinned even more as I felt myself start to blush.

But I was glad to have a minute alone with Logan to say hello, which is about all we got to say, because more clients arrived, via Kristy, in her grandmother's car, the Pink Clinker.

I whipped out my roll book again and checked off the names as more and more people showed up. Jamie Newton arrived and announced that he had to go to the bathroom, and Logan said, "See you later," to me and held his hand out to Jamie. "This way," he told Jamie.

"Nineteen, twenty," I counted off the names and made sure that everyone I'd checked off had actually arrived. Two people to go.

And there they were: Bobby and Alicia Gianelli.

Bobby saw all the activity at the tables and took off at once, shouting, " 'Bye, Mom!" over his shoulder.

Alicia, who had just turned four, stood holding her mother's hand, and she reached with her other hand and locked it in place on her mother's wrist.

"Hi, Mrs. Gianelli. Hi, Alicia," I said, checking off the last two names. I put the roll book away and said, "Welcome to Camp BSC."

"Hi, Mary Anne. It looks like a lot of fun, doesn't it, honey?" Mrs. Gianelli said to Alicia. Alicia didn't answer. She just stared up at her mother with big brown eyes.

"Do you know what a circus is, Alicia?" I asked.

Alicia shifted her gaze from her mother to me. She nodded.

"We're drawing our favorite circus animals today. You want to come with me and help me? I can't make up my mind. An elephant? Do you like elephants?"

"Camels," said Alicia.

"Camels? Camels could be in a circus," I said.

Alicia let go of her mother's hand. I reached out and took Alicia's hand in my own. "Camels would look very good in circus costumes. And you know what, Alicia? See Claudia over there? Claudia is an artist and I bet she could think of some great camel costumes."

We started walking toward the tables, but we hadn't gone three steps before Alicia twisted around. *"Mommy!"* she said in a panicked voice. "Mommy, don't go!"

"Would you like to see the tables and some of the artwork?" I said. "We'll have juice a little later this morning. And we have a surprise announcement this afternoon for all the campers."

I was talking as much to Alicia as to Mrs. Gianelli and Mrs. Gianelli did the same, exclaiming over how much fun everything sounded and laughing at some of the funny hat drawings Claudia came up with for Alicia's camel. Alicia seemed to enjoy it, but I noticed that she kept making eye contact with her mother.

Poor Alicia, I thought. She's afraid to be separated from her mother. "It's okay, Alicia," I said. "Camp BSC is going to be lots and *lots* of fun."

Then Kristy said to me, "Everybody's here. Let's let them color for a little longer, then move on to the next activity. . . . Hi, Mrs. Gianelli. You should see the lion Bobby drew for his circus animal. You will, I guess, because everyone's going to bring their drawings home at the end of the day."

"I suppose I can go now," said Mrs. Gianelli in an undertone.

Kristy looked surprised. "Sure!"

Claudia said, turning so that Alicia couldn't hear her, "I think she's fine now. Don't worry."

Mrs. Gianelli left. I watched her go. "Poor Alicia," I said softly. "It must be so scary to be a little kid and have to be left on her own like this."

"But it's not like Alicia doesn't know us," Claudia said practically. "And it's not like it's the first time her mother has ever left her with one of us."

Alicia had raised her head from her coloring project and was watching her mom's car pull

away. I saw her look down the table toward
where her brother Bobby was sitting. Then she
bent her head over her coloring again.

I reached out and gave her shoulder a
gentle, reassuring pat.

Then Jamie Newton's piece of paper blew
away somehow and I ran to help him catch it
and forgot about Alicia for the time being.

I forgot about Alicia until we decided to
make an excursion to the park, right after the
mid-morning juice (during which, miracu-
lously, no major juice mishaps occurred).

Everyone was instantly excited about the
field trip to the park. "Cool," shouted Haley,
signing rapidly to her brother Matt. (Matt is
deaf. We've all learned some sign language,
but none of us can talk with our hands at top
speed the way Haley and Matt do.)

"Monkey bars, monkey bars, all the way up
to Mars," sang Vanessa Pike. Marilyn Arnold
giggled and added, "Swing high, swing low,
to the park we go!"

That set everybody off. We paired the kids
into buddies and divided the buddies among
us, and set off amid some of the most awful
poetry you've ever heard.

All except Alicia. I saw Hannie Papadakis,
who'd been paired with Alicia, say, "Come
on, Alicia."

"No," I heard a firm, small voice say and I

turned to see Alicia standing by the table where she'd been coloring. Her arms were folded. Her face was turning red.

Mal, who was nearest, turned to her. "Alicia? Don't you want to go to the park?"

"The park, the trees, if you please," I heard Vanessa calling out up ahead.

"No." Alicia's tone was firm, but her voice also sounded a bit shaky. Up ahead, I saw Kristy look back and then slow down. The whole "park train" did the same.

Mal said to her group of campers, which included Karen and Nancy, "Wait a minute." I nodded at the twins, Marilyn and Carolyn, who were standing nearby with Becca and Charlotte, and said, "Hold up, you guys."

I went back to join Mal, who had squatted down beside Alicia. "Alicia, is something wrong?" Mal said. "Do you need to go to the bathroom first?"

"No," said Alicia for the third time. She looked at me. "I have to stay here," she said.

"But don't you want to go to the park?" Mal said. "It'll be fun. We can . . ."

Whatever Mal had been going to say was lost in a truly amazing howl as Alicia opened her mouth and squeezed her eyes shut and began to cry.

"Alicia! What's wrong?"

"Not the park. I cannnn't," was what we heard.

"Are you afraid of something in the park?" asked Mal.

Alicia shook her head. She kept crying.

"Shhhh," I said. "You don't have to go to the park if you don't want to. Shhhh." I grabbed one of the paper napkins I'd stuck in the pocket of my shorts (a good baby-sitter is always prepared) and used the napkin as a tissue. I wiped the tears from Alicia's cheeks.

"Mommy," sniffed Alicia. "What if Mommy comes back for me? What if I'm not here?"

My heart broke for Alicia. She looked so little and scared and forlorn standing there.

"Your mom won't be back until after lunch. This afternoon," said Mal. She held out her arm, and pointed to her watch. "Not until the big hand is on the twelve and the little hand is on the five, see?"

The tears began to well up in Alicia's eyes again. By this time, of course, all of Camp BSC was gathered around us, watching us as if we were a performance of some sort. But some of the campers, I noticed, were also getting restless.

"Will we get to the park at least by dark?" demanded Vanessa.

I said quickly, "I'll tell you what. I'll stay

here with Alicia. You guys can handle the trip to the park without me, can't you?"

"Well," said Kristy. She didn't look happy. Kristy hates it when her plans get changed.

Mal said, "It probably would be a good idea, at least for today."

"Okay," said Kristy. She's stubborn, but when it comes to baby-sitting she knows that being flexible is key.

"Come on, Hannie, you can be our partner," said Karen instantly and Nancy nodded. "Then we'll be the Three Musketeers."

Camp BSC left for the park. Alicia and I watched them go, and then I persuaded Alicia to take a short walk around the barn (but only after I explained to her that we would be able to see her mother from the barn, if her mom arrived).

I couldn't remember being four, but I could certainly sympathize with Alicia. I also admired her single-mindedness. And of course, as an experienced baby-sitter, I knew that what she needed was some time to adjust to camp. Once she saw that her mother was going to come back and get her every day, no matter what, she'd be fine.

Everyone returned from the park in high spirits and with big appetites. We sorted out the lunches (Camp BSC requirement: all lunches had to be labeled by name) and poured out juice and milk. The kids loved eating outside. We all did.

And in spite of the fact that she hadn't gone to the park, Alicia had an appetite to match everybody else's.

After lunch we settled down for a quiet read-aloud storytime. We divided into two groups for reading aloud, and let the older kids choose which stories they wanted to listen to. Jessi and Mal took the four youngest kids, Claire, Alicia, Andrew, and Jamie, inside and read aloud to them, too, and then settled them down for brief naps.

When quiet time was over, we gathered together all the kids and Kristy stood up. "Welcome to Camp BSC," she said.

Linny Papadakis put two fingers to his mouth and gave a shrill whistle. Some of the kids applauded.

Kristy grinned. "Thank you, thank you. Applause is always welcome. And we'll all be getting plenty of applause because we've decided on a theme for Camp BSC. We're going to have a circus camp!"

Karen's hand immediately shot up. "Kristy! Kristy!" Karen called, waving her hand furiously.

"What is it, Karen?" Kristy asked.

"Is this a real circus camp?" Karen asked, her blue eyes intent behind her glasses.

"I'm not sure what you mean," said Kristy.

"I've been to a real circus camp," said Karen. She looked around. "We learned about real circus things."

Ricky Torres was nodding and waving his hand at the same time. "Me, too! Are we going to learn about tightropes? Trapezes?"

"Lion taming?" asked Hannie.

"You didn't learn how to tame lions at circus camp!" exclaimed Claudia. I could tell she was trying not to laugh.

Kristy took charge. "How many kids here have been to circus camp?"

"Real circus camp?" asked Karen.

"Karen," said Kristy warningly. "Everybody who has been to circus camp before, raise your hand."

Karen and Ricky raised their hands. So did Natalie, Chris, Hannie, Linny, Nancy, and Bobby. Bobby said, "I didn't go with Karen. I went to another camp."

"Okay, good." Kristy nodded. "I'm pleased to see we have so many experienced circus campers with us. That will make our circus that much better at the end of the camp. I'm counting on you experienced circus hands to help us out."

"Will we have a tightrope?" persisted Ricky.

"We can learn about tightropes," Kristy

said. "We'll figure out what acts we want to do as we go along."

"No tightropes way up in the air," said Karen. "They wouldn't let us have a tightrope in the *real* circus camp."

"I think circus camp is a great idea," said Becca Ramsey. "Maybe some of us can pretend to be lions and do a lion taming act!"

"Excellent," said Kristy. "I want you to think about all the things you want to do for our circus and come tomorrow ready to write them down. Then we'll decide what we want our circus to have in it.

"Now, let's have a game of freezetag."

Kristy had averted a circus riot. I caught her eye and gave her a thumbs-up signal. Then we all joined in a game of freezetag until the parents started returning to pick up their kids.

The moment the first parent arrived, Alicia froze.

"You haven't been tagged yet," I said to her, since I was standing (frozen) nearby.

"Where's Mommy?" she said. "Where's my mother?"

"She'll be here soon," I promised.

Alicia's lower lip trembled. "I want my mother."

"Alicia," I began.

Alicia's whole face lit up. "Mommy,

Mommy, Mommy!" she shrieked and took off across the yard.

I followed her to make sure everything was all right and watched her fling herself headfirst into her mother's legs.

"Whoa there," Mrs. Gianelli said. She bent down and scooped up Alicia. "How's my girl? Did you have a good day at camp?"

Alicia nodded.

"I'll go get Bobby," I said.

Unlike Alicia, Bobby wanted to stay until he finished the game. With her mother there, Alicia soon wanted to play, too. Mrs. Gianelli stood by me and watched.

"Has Alicia been, uh, separated from you much before?" I asked.

"No," said Mrs. Gianelli cheerfully. "Today was the longest time. I started to come by at lunch to check on her, but then I thought it might make things worse. Did she do okay?"

Claudia, who was standing beside me said, "Her first whole day! Wow. She did super, Mrs. Gianelli. Except she didn't want to go to the park because she was afraid you wouldn't know where to find her if you came back early."

The game of freeze tag was ending since the parents had arrived. Mrs. Gianelli laughed and caught Alicia's hand in her own as Alicia came running back. "I'll try to explain it to her," she promised us.

" 'Bye, guys," called Claudia.

" 'Bye, Bobby. 'Bye, Alicia," I said.

" 'Bye," said Bobby. "See you tomorrow."

"Good-bye," said Alicia. She looked up at her mom. "I don't have to come back tomorrow, do I?" she asked as they were leaving.

Claudia gave a little snort. "I don't think Alicia likes Camp BSC."

Logan had wandered over to us and he bumped his shoulder against mine. "Who doesn't like the best camp in all of Stoneybrook?"

"Alicia," I said. "She's having some adjustment problems."

"Standard stuff," said Claudia. "She'll get over it. You'll see."

"Maybe," I said.

Everyone else had joined us and we automatically went to work, cleaning up after the day's activities and getting things ready for the next day. We didn't talk much. We were all a little tired.

But circus rebellion and Alicia's adjustment problems aside, it had been a pretty good day. It looked as if Camp BSC was going to be a stupendous success.

CHAPTER 5

"No, no, no, noooooo!"

Alicia Gianelli looked like the perfect camper. Her white sneakers were spotless and so were her white socks with lavender trim that matched the lavender stripes on the side of her navy blue shorts. She was wearing a navy and lavender and white striped T-shirt and carrying a safety-orange backpack. Until a moment ago, she'd been holding her lunch in a dinosaur-decorated insulated lunch bag.

But when her mother had turned to go, Alicia had dropped the lunch bag *and* the appearance of being a perfect camper and flung herself at her mother to clutch her knees.

"Noo, don't gooooo!" Alicia wailed.

Poor Alicia. I knew that Mrs. Gianelli had explained about camp to her. So had I. So had Claudia. And Mal. And Jessi. And Dawn. And Kristy. And Shannon. And Logan.

Everyone in the BSC had tried to convince Alicia that she didn't need to worry. That her mother was coming back — just as she had come back every single day, all four days, since Camp BSC had been in session.

Alicia had nodded. And continued to cling to her mother desperately every single day when Mrs. Gianelli had tried to leave Camp BSC.

"Oh, Alicia," I said softly. I bent over and smoothed her soft, dark hair.

Alicia shook her head angrily. *"No!"*

"No way, huh?" asked Mal.

Mrs. Gianelli bent over and unwound Alicia's arms. "Come on, Alicia. I'll walk with you to your table."

Still sniffling, Alicia allowed herself to be led to the table. "We have some new circus books here," said Mal. "Look at this one. It's got a camel in it. You like camels, don't you?"

Alicia reached for the book.

Mal looked up. "I think you can go now," she said softly.

"Well . . ." Mrs. Gianelli hesitated. Nearby, Bobby had already forgotten about his mother and was involved in a lion roaring contest with Ricky.

"You don't have to," I said quickly.

"Neat camel, Alicia," said Claudia, who'd

arrived with some more crayons and paper for Alicia's table. "Want to try to draw one?"

Alicia took the crayons from Claudia and began to sort them into piles of similar colors on the table. Claudia looked up at Mrs. Gianelli. "She'll be fine. Don't worry."

Reassured, Mrs. Gianelli nodded and strode across the grass to her car. Alicia, oblivious to the stains of the tears drying on her cheeks, bent over the crayons and her book, studying them intently.

"Poor Alicia," I said softly to Mal as she stood beside me. "It seems mean to trick her."

"Maybe," said Mal. "But once she starts having a good time, I don't think she really misses her mom all that much. You know, some of that crying and carrying on is probably just habit."

I looked at Mal and shook my head. How could she be so unfeeling? Maybe being the oldest in a large family did that to you.

And she was wrong, as Alicia clearly demonstrated when we got ready for our morning trip to the park.

The moment it was mentioned, Alicia began to cry. "Mommy," she whimpered. "What if Mommy can't find me?"

Bobby, with all the callous superiority of an older brother, said, "You are such a baby, Alicia. You think Mom's dumb? Of course she can find us."

"Bobby!" I said. I bent over and gave Alicia, who was staring at her brother's retreating back, a big hug. "Of course your mommy can find you. But if you don't want to go to the park, you don't have to. We can stay right here."

"Mary Anne." I looked up to see Logan standing beside me.

"What?"

"Do you think that's a good idea?" asked Logan. "Giving in like that?"

Honestly, what was the matter with everybody? I know I'm supposed to be very sensitive, but it only took an average amount of sensitivity, a *human* amount, to realize what Alicia was going through.

Something in my expression must have alerted Logan to how completely indignant I was feeling, because instead of waiting for an answer, he raised one hand. "Just a thought," he said quickly. "Maybe you're right. Maybe she's not ready yet. It'll probably take a little more time."

"Probably," I said shortly.

Everyone else went to the park. Alicia and I stayed behind.

* * *

After the Camp BSCers returned and we'd eaten lunch and had quiet time, we got down to circus business.

"Rehearsals!" Kristy called, holding her clipboard and blowing a whistle. Everyone began to talk at once.

"Roustabouts, over here," said Dawn. "Roustabouts" is the name for circus people who help do all kinds of things. Our roustabouts, Vanessa, Nicky, Linny, Haley, and Carolyn were helping Dawn and Logan move bales of hay to the level field behind the barn where they were setting up the ring.

Jessi gathered the animal dancers together for the animal dance she was helping them choreograph.

Claudia called the wild animals for the wild animal act over to her. She was going to help them work on costumes until the animal trainers — Nicky and Marilyn — had finished being roustabouts.

Kristy and Shannon and the clowns went to the far side of the barn to begin practicing their routine. When Claudia had started the animal costumes, she was going to help the clowns with theirs.

Mal and I were in charge of the specialty acts and costumes. The specialty acts were going to include some of the campers' pets (we were going to have a couple of special "pet days" for the rehearsals). We hadn't quite decided what the other acts were going to be.

But then, some of the campers hadn't quite decided how they were going to fit into the circus. Or even if they wanted to.

There'd been a sort of division in Camp BSC since the first day, a natural division, really. The kids who went to Stoneybrook Academy were hanging out together and choosing each other for sides in kickball games and things like that. And the kids from Stoneybrook Elementary School were doing the same thing. It wasn't really conscious and it wasn't severe. It was just a pattern that we'd noticed, but we had decided to try to keep the kids from getting too entrenched in it.

We'd been assigning different people to be buddies every day, sitting the kids at different tables at lunch, and trying to make sure they didn't divide into cliques. So far, no problem.

Except for one thing. The kids who had gone to circus camp all happened to be Stoneybrook Academy kids. And they were not wildly enthusiastic about the circus idea. Karen had declared the plan babyish and had quickly won over Hannie and Nancy, along with Ricky, Bobby, Natalie, and Chris. They were very vocal about how silly they thought those plans were.

Those were the same kids who were standing in front of me now.

"Okay, guys," said Mal. "Are you all going to be specialty acts? Or what?"

Karen folded her arms. "This is dumb," she said. "Ricky thinks so, too, don't you, Ricky?"

Ricky nodded. Ricky often goes along with Karen.

But then, so do her two other best friends, Nancy and Hannie, who were also nodding. Bobby and Chris didn't look quite so scornful.

"Excellent! Great work, clowns. David Michael, Carolyn. Very natural. It didn't even look like you meant to run into each other!"

Kristy's voice came to us clearly from the side of the barn.

I looked over there and saw Carolyn and David Michael scrambling to their feet. "Uh," David Michael said, "we didn't, exactly."

That didn't faze Kristy. "Oh? Well, keep up the good work. Now, who can do cartwheels? It's very important that we have at least one clown who can do cartwheels . . ."

"*Raaaayrrr*," shrieked Claire. "I'm a wild animal and I'm going to bite you, Andrew. I'm a lion!"

"Well, I'm a giant tiger and I'm bigger than you are!" Andrew shrieked back.

"If you're a giant tiger, we'll have to draw giant tiger whiskers on your face for the circus," Claudia intervened hastily. "Let's draw a picture of what you want your tiger face to look like."

Alicia, I was relieved to note, didn't seem at all disturbed by the wild animal war. She sat calmly next to Jamie, gluing something together.

I turned back to the circus snobs.

"Okay, you guys," Mal was saying. "You don't have to be in the circus. You can just sit quietly and watch everybody practice and make costumes."

Karen frowned.

"Good idea," I said quickly. "We'll set up a special table for all the people who are being left out of the circus. We'll even give you a special place to sit when we put the show on for the parents on the last day of camp."

Karen frowned harder. Then she said, "It's a dumb circus. I guess we'd better be in it just to make sure it isn't too dumb."

"Yeah," said Ricky. I saw his eyes turn toward the circus dancers, who were spinning like tops as Jessi watched. Then he said, "Maybe I could be a dancer."

"Dancers in the circus? That's silly." Karen wrinkled her nose. "You should have a trapeze act."

"You could try out the circus dance and see if you like it, Ricky. If Jessi will let you," said Mal. (Of course, we knew Jessi would let more kids join, but we didn't want to make it seem too easy.)

A moment later, Ricky, Nancy, and Hannie were walking toward Jessi's group.

Karen watched them go. "Dancing," she said scornfully.

Mal said, "Jessi's got a big group over there. Maybe I could help her."

I nodded. I was thinking. "Well, if we can't have a tightrope act, what about a high board act?" I suggested.

Bobby said, "What?"

Looking toward the barn, I watched Logan and Vanessa dragging a bale of hay out of it. "Like with a couple of bales of hay," I said slowly. "We could put a board between a couple of bales of hay and do some balancing tricks on that."

"Oh, brother, how exciting," Karen said sarcastically.

"Karen's right," said Chris. "That's not hard at *all*."

I said, "You can't do them up high, so it won't be exciting to wonder if you're going to fall off. But maybe you could do some cool tricks anyway."

"I guess," Bobby said.

"Let's get a couple of bales of hay and a board and give it a try," I said, leading the three kids toward the barn.

Bobby and Chris ran ahead of me and Dawn waved at them. "Hey. Temporary roustabouts! Give me a hand with this bale."

"We should make a hay carpet from the barn to the circus ring," said Vanessa. "A special circus carpet would be just the thing."

"Good idea," said Logan. He tore some hay from a bale and began to scatter it on the ground.

Carolyn tore some hay from the bale and dropped it on Haley's head.

Linny was one of the kids who'd been to circus camp, but when Dawn had asked for "big, strong" volunteers he hadn't been able to resist. He was helping — reluctantly — but suddenly he dropped his circus snob pose, grabbed another handful of hay, and flung it at Logan.

"Hay fight, hay fight," chanted Nicky happily and plunged in.

For a moment, the hay flew. When Dawn and Logan laughingly called it quits, everyone looked like scarecrows. It made me itch just to look at them.

I was glad I'd managed to stay out of the way of the flying hay.

I wasn't the only one who hadn't gotten

involved. I looked around to see Karen just standing there, a brooding look on her face.

"Have you decided what — if anything — you want to do in the circus?" I asked her.

Narrowing her eyes, Karen shook her head. "I'm thinking!" she said. "I'm thinking!"

CHAPTER 6

"Oh, oh, oh *HI* oh," my father sang, way, *way* off key. I winced and covered my ears but I was laughing.

"That bad, huh?" said Dad. "Okay, I'll stop." He disappeared down the hall. I heard him say, "I know I left my extra pair of brown socks in this drawer."

It was Sunday, the end of the first week of Camp BSC and the day my father was leaving for Cleveland, Ohio. I hadn't forgotten, exactly, but I'd been so busy with Camp BSC that I'd lost track of when he was leaving until Sharon had said something about a special going-away lunch for Dad on Sunday.

"A calling-all-cookbooks blowout feast," Sharon said. "And then it's the last time I stove-wrestle until Richard comes home again."

I'd had to laugh. "You mean you're giving up cooking until then?"

"Until then," she'd agreed. "You want some input on this blowout feast?"

"Definitely," I said.

So now I was headed downstairs to help Dawn set the table and start lunch, which was really a brunch menu: cold poached salmon (Sharon's recipe) with asparagus vinaigrette (we were serving that hot, with Dawn's special oil and vinegar herb dressing). Dawn and I were even making real bread, from the ground up. I hadn't done that before, but Dawn had, back in California.

While the bread was baking and the warm asparagus that we'd just cooked was marinating, Dawn and I set the table and made a bouquet of flowers from the back flowerbed. We had plenty of flowers to choose from. Sharon's gardening is sort of like her housekeeping — a little of this and a little of that thrown together. It made for a colorful flowerbed and a beautiful big bunch of flowers.

Sharon came downstairs and made fresh squeezed orange juice and coffee and even heated the milk for the coffee and put it in a pitcher on the table, just as my father came down the stairs.

"Mmm," he said. "Something smells good."

"Homemade bread," said Dawn, pointing to the basket, where the bread was wrapped in a red and white checkered dishcloth.

"Brunch is served," said Sharon grandly and she escorted Dad to his seat at the table and held his chair for him. That made Dawn and me giggle.

We sat down and ate and talked, and I thought how much I like my family (I often get these thoughts when we are gathered around the dinner table, most often when it is for a special meal).

Then my dad looked at his watch and said, "Time for half a cup more," and shifted into his organized-husband-and-father routine. That meant that between sips of coffee, he went over all the lists of where things were and who to call if something broke and where he would be and what needed to be done while he was away.

Sharon was cool. She didn't remind Dad that she and Dawn and Jeff had lived in the house awhile before Dad got there, so of course she knew where things were and who to call if something broke that she couldn't fix it herself. She thanked Dad for reminding her (twice) to be sure to have the oil changed on the car the moment it had gone another fifty miles.

So Dawn and I nodded and smiled, too, as Dad reminded us to do our chores (as if we hadn't been doing them all along!) and not to get into any trouble. We were careful not to look at each other because we knew we would burst out laughing. Instead we jumped up and started clearing the table.

Sharon went upstairs to help Dad pack and in no time at all he trotted back down the stairs holding his suitbag and suitcase. "Time to hit the road," he announced.

We drove to the airport. Dad reminded Sharon about the oil. Sharon teased Dad about what a wild time we were going to have "baching it" while he was away.

"Just don't forget to call," Dad said.

We were there in plenty of time for his flight, of course. We walked Dad to the metal detector. He hugged us good-bye. I hugged him hard, feeling a sudden, unexpected lump in my throat.

" 'Bye, Dad," I said, swallowing hard and feeling a little misty-eyed.

He gave me another quick squeeze, kissed Sharon, and walked through the metal detector, around the corner, and out of sight.

And suddenly I felt abandoned. Lost. Left behind.

It was so weird. I mean, I knew where Dad was going and I knew when he'd be back and I was looking forward to hanging out with Sharon and Dawn Schafer.

But still. It was a very strong, very unhappy feeling.

Fortunately Dawn and Sharon didn't seem to notice. Sharon stared after my dad for a moment, then turned to face us with a huge smile.

"Surf's up!" she said.

"Aw, Mom," said Dawn, but she was grinning, too. They were in high spirits, and they stayed that way all the way home. I smiled and made myself join in, but I still couldn't shake that little-kid, I-miss-my-dad feeling.

Stop that, I told myself sternly. You are grown-up. You are not Mary Anne the little kid in braids anymore.

But it didn't help.

"Let's have a stupid videos night," said Sharon as we returned to Stoneybrook.

"Great idea," said Dawn.

"Stupid videos?" I asked.

"Yeah, you know, Mary Anne. We'll watch dumb, nonmeaningful videos. Silly ones. Funny ones. And we'll goof on them and eat popcorn."

"And throw it at the screen during the dumbest scenes," Sharon said.

"Oh," I said.

Sharon zipped the car into the parking lot of the Stoneybrook MegaVideo and said, "Okay, we can each choose one video."

Sharon and Dawn went wild in the video store. Oh, not like little kids, running around and screaming or anything. But they would grab a video and say, "Listen to this," and read the back of it aloud to each other. (And to me, at first. But I admit, I felt kind of embarrassed so I slid over to another aisle.)

Dawn chose a video called *Plan Nine From Outer Space*. Sharon found "maximum stupid video potential" in an old Elvis Presley movie called *Girls, Girls, Girls*. I grabbed a movie called *Buffy the Vampire Slayer* at the last minute.

I didn't know if it would qualify or not, but the blues that I'd been feeling ever since my dad had disappeared from sight suddenly made decision-making extremely difficult.

We decided to watch them in alphabetical order (my idea) and *Buffy* wasn't bad. Or maybe I mean it wasn't good. Anyway, we all laughed at it. Then we sent out for Chinese food. In no time at all Chinese food containers were all over the place.

We watched part of the second movie and then we made popcorn. Some of the empty and half-empty Chinese food containers made it back to the kitchen and maybe *one* of them made it into the garbage.

But a lot of them stayed where they'd been set down on the coffee table and the end tables and even on the floor. A lot of popcorn also ended up on the floor, because Sharon had been serious about throwing popcorn at the movie during the parts she didn't like.

"Oh, no!" she shrieked. "Elvis is going to sing!"

She and Dawn launched a storm of popcorn at the television.

"Got him!" Dawn announced, laughing breathlessly. "Right between the eyes! Did you see, Mary Anne?"

"Great shot!" I said, trying to sound as if I were having fun.

But I wasn't. After awhile (as we were watching Elvis look deep into a girl's eyes as he sang) I yawned. "We have a busy day tomorrow," I said.

Sharon replied, "Yes. But that's half the fun of staying up late, isn't it?"

I said, "Well, I think I'll go on to bed."

"Okay." Sharon launched another popcorn attack. "Two handfuls *down* on that scene!" Then she said, "Uh-oh, we're almost out of popcorn."

"I'll make some," said Dawn, standing up. "Quick, pause it until I get back."

"You want me to help clean up before I go to bed?" I asked.

"Oh, don't worry about that, Mary Anne. We're bachelor girls now," said Sharon. "Sleep tight, dear."

"Good night," I said.

"Drag me out of bed in the morning, and don't let me complain, okay?" said Dawn.

"Sure," I said.

I went to bed feeling left out. Dawn and her mother had grown closer since Dawn had returned from California and I was glad of that.

But it made me miss my father even more — and I hadn't expected to miss him at all.

CHAPTER 7

Monday

Dawn, when you suggested that we have a Nature Day, complete with a visit to the Stones' farm, I bet you never expected to meet snakes. And bears. And tigers. And people-eating goats... Not that your fearless BSC leader is afraid of a goat!

Dawn's brilliant idea had been a hit with all the BSC members and the kids. The morning of the hike was spent talking about visiting the Stones' farm and organic farming and all the animals that might live on the Stone farm and in the woods around their house. After lunch, the campers were going to take a Nature Hike, down the road to the Stones' farm. They were going to walk along an old path in the wooded area behind the fields and houses that lined Burnt Hill Road.

Everybody was excited about the trip.

Except Alicia.

Neither Kristy nor anyone else was surprised.

Kristy announced, "Everybody get a buddy for the hike," and a mad scramble ensued.

Except for Alicia. "No," she said.

"But Alicia, we've been talking about this all day," said Dawn.

Alicia blinked rapidly, as if she might be trying not to cry, and I felt sorry for her.

Dawn didn't seem to notice. "Your mom knows where you are. She knows we're going on this trip. Remember? You and Bobby took a note home to your parents that told them about it."

"No," said Alicia.

"You don't remember taking the note home? Or — "

"She doesn't want to go," I said, coming to Alicia's rescue.

"But . . ." Dawn's voice trailed off. She looked at me. "Does that mean you're not coming? That you're going to stay here with her?"

"Of course," I said. "I don't mind. Why make Alicia miserable?"

Kirsty said, "Right," briskly, as if she were washing her hands of the problem. She raised her voice. "Okay, everybody, have you got your partners, your buddies?"

Karen said, "My partner has to be a *real* circus person." She was clearly disgusted because Hannie and Nancy had already decided to be partners.

Fortunately, before anyone's feelings could get hurt, Ricky said, "I'll be your partner, Karen."

"Good," Kristy said. She looked around and saw that Claire's face was turning red and recognized the signs of a tantrum. (Claire doesn't have tantrums as often as she used to, but the signs are still the same: a red face, a lower lip jutting out, and then the shriek of "Note air" — which means no fair.)

"What is it, Claire?" asked Kristy.

"No buddy," said Claire.

"Easy," said Jessi, stepping in. "You can be *my* buddy, Claire."

Claire's pout became a frown, then a smile, and another disaster was averted.

"Everybody fall in," shouted Kristy. She waved good-bye to me and led the way across the field behind our house toward the strip of woods that marched up the hills there. Mrs. Towne owned the field, but she leased it to the Stones who lived farther down the road and they kept it mowed for hay. Right now the field was just sprouting new green grass, and birds were swooping down over it, looking for insects.

They hadn't gone very far when Kristy stopped and pointed upward. "Look! A hawk!"

Everyone stopped and looked into the sky. A hawk was circling above. The BSC members had borrowed binoculars from their parents, ranging from the big clunky ones that Logan's father had owned since he was a kid to a lightweight pair belonging to Watson. The campers all took turns looking at the hawk.

"He's looking at me, he's looking at me," Karen cried. She pulled back from the binoculars, shoved them at Kristy and ducked down behind her. "Don't let him catch me! Don't let him eat me!"

This, of course, provoked panic among the younger campers, until Mal started laughing. "Wouldn't that hawk look silly if he — or she — came down and tried to pick you up? All the other hawks would laugh at him, because they know that hawks never, ever bother people."

"Do hawks laugh?" asked Claire, forgetting to be scared.

"Well, nobody knows for sure, Claire," said Dawn. "But some animals laugh."

"Carrot laughs," said Charlotte Johanssen, talking about her pet schnauzer. "Whenever he's playing and you hold the ball up, his tongue hangs out and he laughs."

"Hyenas laugh," said Haley.

"And cuckoo birds," said Logan.

"What about monkeys?" asked Becca.

The campers made it across the field without any more frights. And the hawk stayed right where he was.

On the trail the kids saw the hoofprints of deer and talked about the spots on fawns that help disguise them. They saw a chipmunk. Marilyn, who has a very good ear, helped identify the song of a cardinal. They checked out the flowers that were growing and the blooms that were on the trees. And then they reached the gate at the end of the field behind the Stones' farmhouse and barns.

Mrs. Stone was expecting everybody, of course. She came out of the barn, wearing overalls and big boots and holding a pitchfork.

"Have you been mucking out stalls?" asked Mal. Mucking out stalls means cleaning them. As a horse fanatic, Mal knows everything there is to know about horses — and their stalls.

"Just moving a little hay around," said Mrs. Stone. "Welcome to our farm, everyone."

"We've been here before," said Carolyn and Marilyn in unison. As usual, they didn't seem to notice when they spoke at exactly the same time.

"So you have," said Mrs. Stone, smiling. "You came with Mary Anne."

"She had to stay home this time. With one of the babies," said Karen scornfully.

"Karen," said Kristy warningly.

"Sorry," said Karen, instantly contrite.

Mrs. Stone looked at her watch. "Mr. Stone will be back in a little while, but in case he gets delayed, why don't we start our tour of the farm. We'll start with the barn. It's a lot like the barn at Mary Anne and Dawn's. In fact, the basic structure was built at about the same time. But this barn has changed a bit over the years because it's been used steadily since the seventeen hundreds, which means that it has to be repaired and repainted and so forth."

The twenty-one campers and seven baby-sitters stepped into the coolness of the huge old barn behind Mrs. Stone and she showed them the hayloft and explained about storing hay and what it was used for. She let everyone pat the soft noses of two of the cows who were in the barn. "They're about ready to have their calves and we wanted them close by to keep an eye on them," she explained. "We're not a cattle farm, we're a produce farm, but we keep a few heads of cattle for milk and butter and to sell the calves. We sell the extra milk and butter, too."

"You keep the *heads* of cows?" a voice said worriedly.

Mrs. Stone laughed. "Now who asked that question?"

"Me," said Jamie. "Jamie."

"Hi, Jamie. No, not the heads. Head is just a way of referring to the animal. Of counting. Three heads of cattle means three cows."

"Oh." Jamie looked *very* relieved.

Mrs. Stone showed everyone the tractor and the old plow that the tractor had replaced. She explained how hay was baled and how cows were milked.

When we went outside again, she let everyone throw a handful of feed down for the chickens that were scattered around the barnyard.

"We did this before, too," said Marilyn. Carolyn nodded.

"Can chickens be in a circus?" asked Claire.

"Of course not," said Ricky. "Don't you know anything about circuses?"

"No, she doesn't," Hannie whispered loudly to Nancy. "She hasn't been to a *real* circus camp."

Mrs. Stone said, "I've never seen a chicken in a circus, but I suppose one might be. Pigs have been in circuses, you know."

She led the way to the pigpen, where a mother pig and her babies were lying contentedly in the mud.

"Peeee-uuuuuu," cried Bobby.

"Pigs are really very clean animals," said Kristy. "They lie in the mud to keep cool and to keep flies off."

"Right, Kristy. And they are smart," added Mrs. Stone. "They are considered some of the smartest animals in the world, and in ancient times were taught tricks and treated as performing animals."

"Maybe we could borrow a pig for our circus," said Haley.

Kristy quickly stepped in and put a stop to that idea, then let the campers tell Mrs. Stone about the upcoming circus as she led them toward the goat pen.

Naturally, the kids who'd been to circus camp remained aloof, after making it clear that they'd been to a "real" circus camp.

However, the circus camp rivalries were forgotten when the group reached Elvira's enclosure.

Elvira Stone, the world's cutest baby goat (but growing rapidly) and a former babysitting (goat-sitting?) charge, came bounding up to the fence. She was used to visitors and knew that visitors meant being admired and petted and maybe even fed some treats.

She wasn't wrong. Everyone crowded around and asked Mrs. Stone a million questions about Elvira. Mal even asked if it was true that goats eat tin cans.

"I've never seen a goat eat a tin can," said Mrs. Stone. "But they will take a nibble on almost anythi — "

"Aaaughh! Aaaughh! Help! I'm being eaten by a goat!"

Claire Pike came leaping through the crowd. There was a tearing sound.

"Baaaahhh," said Elvira, trying to follow Claire.

"Save me, save me!" shrieked Claire, ducking behind Jessi.

Dawn reached out and caught Elvira by

wrapping one arm around her neck. Thinking she was being hugged (and more or less right about it), Elvira stopped immediately — all except her jaw, which kept working. A short strip of cotton T-shirt was hanging out of her mouth like a blue tongue.

Claire looked out from behind Jessi.

"Oops," said Mal. "Looks like you're going to get a new shirt, Claire."

Some of the kids started to laugh. Claire looked around. Her face grew red.

Elvira stood there, chewing, until Mrs. Stone reached out and took the little strip of blue cloth from her mouth.

Then Claire started to laugh. "I got eaten by a goat."

Of course, Matt and David Michael and the other kids immediately started sticking their arms out and the tails of their shirts to see if Elvira would sample those.

And of course, the members of the BSC hustled them quickly on to the next segment of the nature walk.

They listened as Mrs. Stone explained about organic farming and why the Stone family farm was being converted to an organic farm.

They laughed at Screaming Yellow Honker, the watch goose.

But all they talked about, all the way home, was how Claire had been eaten by a goat.

CHAPTER 8

M_y father had been gone four whole days.

I wasn't counting the days until he came back. But I was surprised by how much I missed him. It's funny how you don't miss something until it's gone. Dawn is one of my two best friends and I miss her when she goes to California. I always tell people that I don't miss my mother because she died when I was just a baby and because I can't really remember anything about her. I think I missed the idea of having a mother more than my actual mother.

But I'd never thought about missing my father. I mean, he'd been away on business trips before, when I was growing up. I'd stayed with weird baby-sitters and with my friends. When I stayed with the weird baby-sitters, I missed him a lot, and when I stayed with my friends Kristy and Claudia, I didn't miss him so much.

Since Dad and Sharon had gotten married, though, he hadn't been away except on a couple of overnight trips for his firm. I'd gotten used to my new family. I'd gotten used to being even closer to my dad, too, now that I was growing up and he didn't treat me like such a child anymore.

I hadn't realized that, but it was true. I was closer to my dad than I had ever been. As close to my dad as Dawn was to her mother.

And I was as much like my dad in many ways as Dawn was like her mom.

Okay, I'm not the neat freak that my dad is. In fact, Dawn probably keeps her room just as neat as mine and maybe a little neater. With each passing day, however, I noticed myself doing things more and more like my father, and saying things that he would say. Almost as if, by acting like him, he would seem to be around more.

The first night, the Chinese food night, was only the beginning. From there, it was take-out food every night: pizza, tex-mex, a vegetarian feast from the Tofu Express.

Dawn or Sharon always told the people not to pack the food in Styrofoam, and not to send plastic forks.

But that didn't mean that the little foil containers that were supposed to be washed and recycled got washed and recycled. At best they made it as far as the sink where they were "put in to soak." Which meant they were filled up with water and left there.

No plastic utensils? We used up all the silverware. Then Sharon dug out the "good silver" and we started using that. It didn't take long for her to take out the "good plates," too.

And the kitchen bulletin board had disappeared under the collection of take-out menus. Sharon brought them home from work. We looked up new places that delivered food and ordered from them and *they* brought more food. If Dawn hadn't been so caught up in Camp BSC, she might have scouted Stoneybrook for even more take-out menus.

I didn't know there were so many places that delivered in the whole world, and especially not right here in Stoneybrook.

Do I sound cranky? I was. Partly because I'd gotten used to home-cooking, Schafer-Spier style. It sounds corny, I know, but I liked those evenings in the kitchen making dinner with Dawn or Sharon or my dad. I liked the times the menu planning was up to me and I could come up with whatever I wanted (except meat, of course). I liked seeing what new vegetarian delight Dawn was going to invent. If it hadn't been for Dawn, I might never have appreciated three-cheese macaroni, or tofu. (Although, like Kristy, I never could and never will appreciate sprouts. She's right when she says they look like green hair and they *are* disgusting and embarrassing when they get stuck in your teeth.)

I tried cleaning up the house. I sorted junk mail and magazines and old newspapers into the recycling bins from the huge piles that Dawn and Sharon were letting collect in the mud room. I ran about a thousand loads of dishes in the dishwasher, trying to keep up. I wiped countertops. I put toilet paper on the toilet paper rolls instead of letting it sit around on places like the edge of the bathtub where it was sure to fall in when someone was taking a shower. (It did. To me.)

I'd been pulled into the role of Maid Mary Anne once before, and I hadn't liked it then. I didn't like it now, either. On the other hand, no one was asking me to clean up. No one even seemed to care.

As the week drew to an end, I felt tense, cranky, and if we'd been having a real circus, I would have been the people-eating tiger. I felt completely out of it. Dawn had turned into some kind of alien house-destroyer and take-out fiend. I missed my father, and the fact that he called every night didn't help. I'd asked him, casually, if there was any way that he could come home sooner.

He'd laughed. "I know my three girls are

living a wild bachelor life. You can't fool me."

I'd laughed too. Weakly.

Dad had gone on, "I miss you. I'll get home as soon as possible."

"I miss you, too," I'd told him. After I'd hung up the phone, I scooped Tigger up and went to bed. Downstairs I heard Dawn and Sharon talking and laughing.

Tigger purred on the bed. At least he was happy, I thought.

I felt worse than ever. The next day couldn't come soon enough.

"What was I going to do? What . . ." Karen put her finger on her chin and tapped it thoughtfully. At any other time, I would have been amused. It was such an adult gesture, so clearly copied from someone else. I'd wondered if her father did it. Or her mother. Or her teacher.

Then she looked at me. "Oh, yes. Now I remember. I was going to do a *real* circus trick. I'd like to work on my props, but I need someplace gigundoly private."

"I'll pull one of the smaller tables around to the other side of the big tree. How's that?" I asked.

"Fine, thank you," said Karen.

I got Karen settled. (She put her bulging backpack on the table in front of her, and waited pointedly until I walked away.) Then I rejoined Claudia. She and I were overseeing some of the campers who were putting finishing touches on their costumes. The clowns had tie-dyed and painted oversized old T-shirts and pants into gaudy, multicolored costumes. Some of them were painting old sneakers, too. The animal doctors and wild animals were securing tails on leotards and making lions' manes out of yarn and fabric scraps.

Out of the corner of my eye I could see Bobby and Chris practicing their high-board act with Kristy's help. From behind the barn I noticed Hannie sewing big white felt claws onto fuzzy black gloves to make the paws of her bear costume. I heard Hannie say to Nancy, "It's too bad we can't have some real circus acts."

"Yeah," said Nancy. "But this isn't a real circus camp, Hannie. Just a, just a . . . you know." She shrugged her shoulders.

Claudia looked up. I could tell she was annoyed. But before she could say anything, Carolyn said, "This is a real camp. We're even going to have a cookout tomorrow night. It's fun. I like it."

"Don't you like this camp?" asked Becca.

"Well, sure. I guess. I mean . . ." Hannie's voice trailed off. She looked confused.

"Why don't you like this camp?" persisted Becca. "Just because you're not at circus camp doesn't mean you can't have fun at this camp. It's just a different camp, that's all."

Hannie said, "Maybe." She quickly bent over her paws again.

Claudia said, "Thank you, Becca, Carolyn."

"For what?" asked Becca. Carolyn looked puzzled.

"For being cool kids," said Claudia. "In fact, you are all cool kids. And we are going to have a one hundred percent cool circus. Okay?"

Nancy and Hannie looked up and exchanged glances. Then Nancy smiled. "Okay," she said.

"How are you doing, Alicia?" I asked softly, resting my hand on her shoulder.

"Okay." Alicia barely even looked up from the special "camel decorations" she was gluing together. As it turned out, Alicia already had a camel costume from Halloween. But she was making new and beautiful circus accessories for her camel to wear in the wild animal act. Andrew and Claire were going to be lions and Jamie was going to be a tiger, but Alicia had insisted on being a camel.

Feeling oddly rejected, I wandered back toward Karen.

Immediately she gasped dramatically and flung her body across the prop on which she was working. "You can't see it yet! Go away!" she said.

"Fine," I snapped. It was a good thing Camp BSC was almost over for the week. Because I was clearly a candidate for the crankiest camper award.

After Camp BSC was finished for the day, Dawn said, "Let's hang out on the steps for awhile."

I shook my head. "I'm kind of tired."

I went to my room (trying to ignore the chaos I passed) and closed my door and lay on my bed. I stayed there until Sharon came home and it was time for dinner.

"Only one more day to go in the work week," she sang as I walked into the kitchen. "Let's do something extravagant."

"Clean the kitchen?" I muttered.

Dawn heard me and gave me a puzzled look, but Sharon didn't. "We'll order take-out and since we're using the good china and the good silver, we'll light candles and get out the fancy tablecloth and everything."

"Great idea," said Dawn. "Can we have pizza again?"

"Pizza it is — unless . . . Mary Anne, what would you like?"

"Go on and order pizza," I said. "Whatever."

I took some hamburger out of the freezer (my father called it the Spier emergency hamburger stash). I thawed it in the microwave. I made a salad.

The pizza arrived and Sharon dashed to the door and dashed back again, holding it aloft.

"Mmm," said Dawn. "This is great. Pizza twice in one week. A person can never have too much pizza."

"Maybe," I said.

Dawn looked at my hamburger and said, "Maybe so." She grinned. "I'll snag the ketchup and mustard out of the fridge and put it on the table for you."

When I carried my hamburger and salad into the dining room, the candles were lit and the tablecloth was spread and the good china and silver were set out. It looked very elegant — except for the large pizza with olives, mushrooms, green peppers, onions, eggplant, and garlic in the middle of the table.

Sharon and Dawn cut huge slices and then Sharon raised her slice up. "Here's to the bachelor girls," she said. "And to the magical question no bachelor girl should ever forget."

Then she and Dawn said in unison, "Do you deliver?"

They cracked up. I raised a forkful of salad in a sort of toast, too, so I wouldn't seem like a spoilsport.

But my heart wasn't in it.

Not that anyone noticed. Or cared.

CHAPTER 9

Friday

I don't believe in ghosts (sorry, Dawn) or ghost stories. (Although a lot of guys on my baseball team do. They just won't admit it.) But it's amazing how, when you get enough people together telling scary stories, you can scare yourself anyway. Sometimes I think little kids are a lot tougher than I am. I mean, where did they hear some of those scary stories they were telling?

The Camp BSC cookout for all campers ages seven and up was a success from the moment it was mentioned. Whether the kids were SMSers or SESers, "real" circus camp graduates or beginners, they all stayed on after five-thirty for the cookout. A temporary camper had also joined the group: Jackie Rodowsky (the walking disaster). His parents had called the BSC to see if they could take on a baby-sitting job that night (the Rodowskys had been away on vacation). Of course the BSC had said yes. Jackie's good for a disaster or two on almost any occasion, but he's a super kid.

So with Jackie's help, the campers pitched in. They enthusiastically dug a shallow space in the ground and cleared away the grass and anything that might catch fire around it. They helped look for twigs and small branches so the fire would start. They helped haul logs to put on top of the fire so it would burn longer.

They helped carry the cookout food to the table Dawn and I had pulled up near to where the campfire was going to be (Jackie dropped the napkins in the dirt but no one seemed to mind).

And they cheered when Sharon arrived home, because that meant that now the campfire could be lit and the cookout could begin.

The menu was pretty simple: hot dogs (turkey dogs, actually, because Dawn wouldn't eat beef or pork hot dogs and the kids wouldn't notice the difference anyway), baked beans, coleslaw, and for dessert, s'mores.

"Do you tell good ghost stories?" Ricky asked Logan. Logan was sticking hot dogs onto skewers and showing the campers how to hold them over the fire.

"I do," said Logan. Then he wondered if the stories he was thinking of telling were maybe too scary. "Sort of," he added.

Ricky looked disappointed. "Do you believe in ghosts?"

"Wellll, not exactly," said Logan, not wanting to disappoint Ricky any further. "What about you?"

Ricky's eyes grew very big. "Yes!" he exclaimed.

"Ghosts are *everywhere*," said Karen, taking a hot dog. She looked over her shoulder. "There are even ghosts who eat hot dogs!"

"Not here there aren't," said Logan firmly. He'd encountered Karen's world-class imagination before.

"But we are going to tell ghost stories, aren't we? You always tell ghost stories at camp," Jackie insisted. Jackie was slowly turning his hot dog into a blackened, bubbly mess that, to Logan's eyes, looked like something out of a ghost story. Or a horror film. Deciding that it might *not* be a Jackie disaster in the making, Logan said, "Um, yeah, sure, Jackie."

"Of course we are," said Kristy. "We're a real camp. Real camps always have cookouts and they always have ghost stories at the cookout."

If Kristy was expecting a challenge from Karen or one of the other "real circus camp kids," she didn't get it. Everyone was busy concentrating on their hot dogs and not spilling too much coleslaw and baked beans around on the ground. Jackie ate his blackened hot dog and smacked his lips. "Mmmmm," he said. He gestured and baked beans flew off his plate.

"Too bad we couldn't bring Pow," said Nicky, looking at the coleslaw he'd just dumped off his own plate accidentally. "He's a great vacuum cleaner when you spill something."

"Noodle, too," said Hannie.

Charlotte shook her head. "Carrot won't eat anything until you tell him to."

"Shannon will steal food right off your plate when you aren't looking," David Michael told everyone proudly.

Kristy rolled her eyes.

Shannon (the person, not the dog) said, "Yes, Bernese mountain dogs are very smart.

That's why it's important to train them carefully."

Kristy rolled her eyes again, but she was grinning.

When all the campers had eaten their dinners and helped clear things away, it was time for games. It had been a long day and everyone had eaten a lot, so the games were easy, relatively quiet ones. Logan led a round of Simon Says. Then the campers and the counselors sat in a circle and played a game of Gossip. Claudia whispered a crazy sentence into Marilyn's ear, who was sitting next to her, who whispered it to the next person. When it came to Matt, Haley, who was sitting next to him, signed something quickly. Matt looked surprised, then laughed. He signed something to Jessi, who was sitting next to him on the other side.

"Really?" said Jessi. "Okay." She leaned over and whispered into David Michael's ear.

Of course, the sentence was completely twisted around by then. What Claudia had whispered was, "Hats are nice on sunny days." But the sentence ended up as "Cats like mice and bunnies, please."

Then Ricky said, "Ghost stories! Ghost stories!"

"It's not dark enough yet," objected Karen.

The longer summer day was still very bright. The sun was just beginning to go down.

Natalie looked nervously over her shoulder. "How dark is it supposed to be?"

"We'll tell the ghost stories in the barn," said Dawn, jumping up. "That way it will be dark, but it will still be light outside."

But first some of the campers insisted on putting on their pajamas which they had brought so they could pretend that the cookout was a *real* campout. They looked pretty cute, too.

As we headed for the barn, Karen cleared her throat loudly.

"What about the," Karen lowered her voice to a loud whisper, "Barn Ghost."

"It doesn't come out until after midnight," said Logan quickly. "That's hours from now. You'll be at home asleep. And," he added, anticipating Karen's next comment, "the ghost can't follow you home. It can't leave the barn. It's only the ghost of a barn mouse, you see. A small mouse."

Giggling and talking, the campers went into the barn. Dawn and I had pulled out old blankets and sleeping bags and pillows to spread around on the hay in the barn, and the kids sat on those.

Logan sat next to me and nudged my shoulder with his. I smiled. Having Logan near made me feel a little better, a little less lonely and left out. I knew he sensed that I wasn't feeling good about something. But I also knew he'd wait for me to tell him.

And I wasn't sure there was anything I could tell him.

Dawn lit a lantern and set it in the middle of the ring of campers while Kristy slid the barn door almost shut.

Immediately the barn grew much darker.

Karen whipped a flashlight out of her backpack, turned it on, and held it under her chin. It made her face look scary and her glasses look shiny and ghostly in an owl-like way.

"*Ooooooh*," moaned Karen.

Kristy held up her hands. "Let the ghost stories beginnnnnnn," she intoned in a creepy voice.

Everyone giggled and whispered and snuggled closer to one another.

Logan cleared his throat. "Okay," he said. "Once upon a time there was a man who always wore a yellow ribbon around his throat . . ."

"And when he took the yellow ribbon off his head fell off," said Charlotte briskly. "We all know that one. Tell us something good and *scary*."

"Yeah," said Ricky. "*Super* scary."

Logan was speechless.

Claudia giggled.

Then Mal cleared her throat. She told a ghost story that really was chilling. She filled it with bloody footprints and headless people. And she ended it with everybody dying.

We looked at Mallory in amazement. Was she able to tell such a gruesome story because she was going to be a writer? Or had growing up in the Pike family given her a ghost-storytelling edge?

But if Mal's fellow counselors were disconcerted, none of the campers were. "Oooh," said Karen. "That was a good one!"

Logan stood up and whispered something in Kristy's ear. She looked thoughtful. Then both of them stood up and stepped away from the ghost-story circle.

When they returned, Karen was in the midst of a standard Karen-brand ghost story, full of wild flights of imagination and extra scary details, involving a cave full of vampire bats and a man whose digital watch kept beeping.

After that, we all took turns telling truly gruesome ghost stories. I told one about a ghostly cat (something that had sort of happened to Dawn). Some of the others were so outrageous that they were funny. The campers shrieked — and giggled.

Logan leaned over. "I'll be back in just a minute." I nodded, caught up in the ghost-story spell.

Then Kristy looked at her watch. "Time for one more story. Then we're going to make s'mores and then it's time for everyone to go home."

Silence fell over the group.

Kristy said, "Once upon a time, there was a ghost that hated cookouts. In life, he'd never been allowed to go to camp. He'd always had to stay home. So when he became a ghost, he vowed that he would haunt camps and cook-outs forever. One night, he saw a group of campers go into an old, old barn . . ."

"No!" squeaked Natalie, in a thrilled tone of voice.

Kristy's voice sank to a whisper. "Yes."

Suddenly, a strange moan came from the back of the barn.

"Who's there?" cried Kristy, jumping up.

All the kids leaped to their feet, too.

And Logan leaped out from behind the edge of an old stall.

"*Eeeeeh,*" several kids cried out.

Several others began to laugh.

"Gotcha!" said Logan.

"That was *great*," said Karen.

"Good one, Logan," said Kristy. "Great idea!"

Everyone began to laugh and talk at once. Dawn blew out the lantern carefully. The campers and counselors went back outside. (Sharon had been keeping an eye on the campfire from the house.)

The s'mores were excellent. Logan helped Jackie assemble a double chocolate, single marshmallow s'more (with the marshmallow totally blackened). He helped Matt make a s'more out of Reese's Pieces that Matt had brought just for the occasion. He made a couple of chocolate-only s'mores with the marshmallows on the side.

And he ate about a zillion marshmallows himself. He said he felt a little like he imagined Pow might have felt if Pow had come to the cookout.

Soon it was time for the kids to leave. One by one the campers' parents arrived. Jackie went home with Kristy and Karen and David Michael and Andrew. His mother would pick him up at the Brewers' house later.

Logan went home still laughing to himself. He'd been afraid he was going to scare the campers to death with his story. And even when the story had been a bust, he'd been worried that his idea to "haunt" the barn would be too scary.

But he'd been wrong. The members of Camp BSC — and Jackie Rodowsky — were a lot cooler than he'd given them credit for.

In fact, Logan said, he almost felt sorry for any ghost that they might ever happen to meet!

CHAPTER 10

"Hey, campfire ghost!" called Dawn, waving. She and I were sitting on the front porch the afternoon after the cookout. It was a hot July day and Dawn had turned her face up to the sun. I pulled on a cap, but I was enjoying the sun, too. And enjoying not doing much of anything.

Although I admit that I couldn't help thinking there was a lot that Dawn and I could be doing. Such as cleaning the house.

My dad would be home in another week. Was a week enough time to get the house back in shape?

But the appearance of Logan, riding his bicycle up our driveway, banished the dark thoughts of housework from my mind.

"Logan!" I said.

"You guys ready?" he asked.

"We're wearing our swimsuits under our

clothes and we've got towels in our back-packs," I reported.

"Excellent," said Logan.

We were going to have a long, lazy day, hanging out and riding our bikes around Stoneybrook, ending up at the town pool for a swim. As we pedaled down Burnt Hill Road I began to relax.

We cruised along some of the quieter roads in Stoneybrook. People were out gardening and mowing lawns and reading the newspaper in hammocks and washing cars and walking dogs.

"What a wonderful day!" I called back to Logan and Dawn. "What a wonderful, beautiful day."

"Mary Anne!" Logan shouted.

"Logan!" I shouted back. "Hooray for the day!"

"Mary Anne!" Logan and Dawn shouted at once. "Look out!"

It was too late. I looked down just as the front wheel of my bike was swallowed by an enormous pothole. The wheel bounced down. It bounced up. I wrenched the handlebars sideways, trying to maintain control of the bike. Then the back wheel hit the pothole, bounced out, and propelled the bike into a tree.

It rebounded off that, veered sideways, and flipped over onto the sidewalk, with me underneath.

I don't remember exactly what happened next. I do remember my foot hitting the ground hard as the bicycle skidded and then fell over. I remember landing with a thud on my side and sliding a little ways on the sidewalk.

I remember that it all seemed to happen in super slow motion.

Then I heard Logan saying, "Mary Anne, Mary Anne! Are you all right? Are you hurt?"

"Don't move her," Dawn's voice said.

"Mary Anne, did you hit your head?"

"N-no," I said.

"Can you move your fingers and toes?" asked Dawn.

I experimented gingerly. "Yes." Then I groaned. "Owww. My leg hurts."

"You're all scraped up," said Logan. "I don't think you should move."

I didn't feel like arguing because I didn't feel like moving. I felt more like crying. Instead I closed my eyes as Logan and Dawn lifted the bicycle off of me.

Then I heard a familiar voice say, "What happened? Do you kids need some help?"

"Mr. Braddock," said Dawn. "Mary Anne's

bike hit a pothole and she fell off and we don't know how badly she's hurt."

"We don't *think* it's serious," said Logan quickly and I knew he was trying to reassure me. "She didn't hit her head."

I opened my eyes to show Mr. Braddock I was still conscious. Logan smiled down at me and patted my hand.

Mr. Braddock said, "Still, better not take any chances. Let's take you over to the hospital, Mary Anne. It's a good thing I'm in the station wagon today."

Mr. Braddock's voice faded away. I closed my eyes again. I listened to the clatter of bicycles being loaded into the back of the station wagon. I heard Logan say, "We can all fit up front and Mary Anne can lie in the backseat."

A minute later, Mr. Braddock was bending over me. "We're going to get on either side of you and help you up, very slowly. If anything hurts suddenly, or you feel any sharp pain, let us know at once."

Together the three of them lifted me up. I didn't feel any sharp pains, just an all-over ache and burning sensation along my knees and calves — until I was standing up. "Owww," I moaned. "My leg. My foot."

"Put your arms over our shoulders. Logan, you get the door. Dawn and I are going to carry you to the car. Don't put any weight on your left leg."

And that's what they did. I slid gratefully into the backseat and closed my eyes again. I kept them closed until we reached the hospital.

The emergency room physician's assistant asked me a few questions about the accident and did a quick examination. Then I was put on a high gurney and wheeled into a room off to one side.

"She doesn't seem badly hurt. And we should be able to get to her fairly quickly," said the assistant."

"I'll call Mom," I heard Dawn say. "She's my sister."

"May I stay with her?" asked Logan.

"For the time being," said the assistant. "But you must leave when we tell you to."

"I will," Logan promised.

A moment later, I felt Logan take my hand. "Don't worry. Everything will be okay."

I opened my eyes and smiled at him. My whole body ached and my ankle was starting to throb ferociously. And more than anything else in the world, I wanted my father.

But of course Dad couldn't come. And Logan was right. Everything was okay.

Sharon arrived in no time at all and took

charge of things expertly. When Logan and Dawn were banished to the waiting room, Sharon stayed with me. The doctor checked me over and asked me more questions, and then Sharon asked her at least half a dozen. Then there were X-rays and another consultation, this time with the physician's assistant.

"We've taken a look at the X-rays," he said. "No bones are broken, no serious injuries. Just a lot of painful scrapes and bruises that initially made things look worse than they are. And a badly sprained ankle. We're going to take off the temporary dressings on the abrasions and contusions and we're going to put that ankle in a soft brace and try to get you on your way as soon as possible."

He worked quickly and efficiently, I'm sure, but it seemed to take forever. I thought I was going to faint when he started work on my ankle. Tears came to my eyes and Sharon, who'd been sitting next to me, slipped a warm hand into mine. "Squeeze my hand," she said. "It'll help."

So I did. I must have practically broken her hand, but she never said a word. And when I was done, she told me she was proud of me for staying so calm.

She also wrote down all of the doctor's instructions and made sure that the nurse was going to wheel me and my new crutches to the door of the emergency room and help settle me comfortably in the car.

I slept for several hours when I got home. When I woke up, Sharon and Dawn helped me limp from my room to the telephone. I called Dad and told him what had happened.

"Mary Anne! You're not badly hurt? No concussion? Did you hit your head?"

"No, they checked everything," I assured him. "It's a sprained ankle and lots of scrapes and bruises. A badly sprained ankle and lots and *lots* of scrapes. . . . Can you come home now, Daddy?"

I almost never call him Daddy anymore.

I heard my father hesitate. Then he said, "Sweetheart, is Sharon there? May I speak to her?"

Putting my hand over the mouthpiece, I called Sharon to the phone. She wasn't far away, just in the next room to give me some privacy while I talked to my dad.

"Hello, Richard," she said, her voice loving and calm. She listened a moment, then looked over at me and smiled slightly, smoothing my hair back.

"She was very brave. And she's going to be just fine. Don't worry, I have everything well in hand. And with Dawn as a first-class nurse and Mary Anne being such a good patient, there's not a thing to worry about. . . . No, we're going to take her to her doctor in a few days. . . . Yes."

I turned away, disappointed and fuming. I was hurt. Couldn't my father tell how hurt I was? Didn't he care? Was this the reward I got for being brave and calm in an emergency?

Tears stung my eyes. Quickly I slid the crutches back into place and turned toward my room.

Sharon said, "Just a minute, Richard. Mary Anne, do you want to say good-bye to your father? Do you want Dawn to help you back to your room?"

"No! I said good-bye. And I don't need help. I'll just go bravely to my room alone." I said the last sentence under my breath so that Sharon couldn't hear me.

Without waiting for her answer, I thumped and bumped clumsily back to my room and fell into bed.

When Dawn and Sharon came to say good night, I pretended to be asleep.

But I wasn't. It was a long, long time before I fell asleep, long after Tigger had come to claim his place on the end of the bed, long after Dawn and Sharon had gone to bed, too.

I stayed awake and felt lonely and sorry for myself.

CHAPTER 11

Woe! Bowlling is an excelently fun sport.
Especialy when you play with kids. They
are so funy. Even with the kid-sized
bowlling balls, I kept expectting them to
go right down the allie and into the pens.

Claudia counted the pairs of buddies and came up with ten pairs and one extra, as usual. This time it was Jamie.

"Yea, Jamie!" she exclaimed. "I get to have you for my partner. Outstanding!"

Jamie, who'd been looking a little forlorn, suddenly lit up like a Christmas tree. "Oh, boy!" he said. He slipped his hand into Claudia's and looked up with a big Jamie-special smile.

Alicia, who was standing by me, said, "Is bowling fun? I've never been bowling."

"Bowling's *great*, I can hardly wait," Vanessa replied. "I'm glad that Camp BSC made Monday bowling day and included *me!*"

She skipped off with Haley to get in line under Kristy's eagle eye. Then Kristy and Shannon and Logan and Mal and Claudia and Jessi divided up the kids among the three station wagons (the Braddocks', the Pikes', and the Ramseys') and began hustling them into the cars for the afternoon bowling excursion.

"They're going to have lots of fun, aren't they?" asked Alicia.

"Yes. Probably," I said. I couldn't have gone bowling even if I'd wanted to. Not with my dumb ankle in a dumb brace.

Alicia watched as Kristy went from car to car, taking one last head count. Then Alicia said, "Mary Anne, am I going to stay here with you?"

"Sure," I said reassuringly. "Of course. You can keep me company since I can't bowl. . . . I know, let's put some extra-special touches on your camel costume."

I turned and began to crutch-hobble my way across the grass toward the activities tables.

Then I realized that Alicia wasn't with me. I looked over my shoulder. Alicia was standing where I had left her, staring after the departing station wagons.

"Alicia? Alicia!" I called.

At last, slowly, Alicia turned and walked across the grass toward me.

In Claudia's car, Vanesa burst into song. "Hi ho, hi ho, it's off to bowl we go!" Soon everyone in the car had joined in. From there they moved on to "Bowl, bowl, bowl your boat," which sent them into giggles.

Then Claudia thought of "Take Me Out to the Bowl Game," and they sang a few rounds of that.

By the time their car reached the bowling alley, it seemed as if every song in the world had been sung with the word "bowl" in it.

Mr. Braddock grinned and shook his head as he helped Claudia and Mal make sure all the kids got into the bowling alley. For a little while it was chaos as the sitters and the three chaperons, Mr. Braddock, Jessi's Aunt Cecelia, and Mrs. Pike, checked to see that everyone got the right size bowling shoes and bowling balls, that everyone wore socks with their shoes, and that the kids were divided up evenly among the bowling alleys.

Kristy, of course, being the organizer of the world, had called the bowling alley in advance and reserved enough lanes at the far end of the alley away from the other bowlers to minimize the disturbance. Fortunately, it wasn't very crowded at that time of day on a Monday anyway, although there was a group of women who were really knocking down the pins nearby.

But getting everyone to their alleys wasn't the same as getting the bowling underway.

"I can't pick up the ball with my fingers in the bowling ball holes," Jamie gasped, his face red.

"Just hold it in your hands. Like this, see?" Claudia cradled the ball in her hands.

"But then I can't throw it the way everyone else is throwing it!"

"Not everyone is throwing it that way," Mal pointed out. "Claire and Andrew aren't, are you?"

Mal and Claudia were in charge of the three youngest kids.

"I don't know *how* to hold it," said Claire.

Andrew shook his head to show that he didn't either.

"Go for it, Claud," said Mal, grinning. She stepped aside and motioned toward the bowling lane.

Claudia thought, Oh, well, and went for it. Cradling the bowling ball (which was one of the lightweight ones for kids and for some reason was bright red) in both hands, she walked to the edge of the bowling alley, bent over, and set it down. Then she gave it a push.

The ball rolled slowly down the alley for a little ways, then curved off into the gutter.

Claire said, "I don't want my bowling ball to do *that!*"

"It might, though," Mal said, trying not to laugh. "But you'll have to practice. Just like you practice softball."

"Oh." Claire could understand that.

Next to them, Matt, David Michael, Ricky, and Bobby were rolling the ball as hard as they could down the alley. Sometimes it actually made it to the pins, but more often it shot into the gutter. Kristy, who was a pretty good bowler, was trying to give them tips on how to hold the ball. But they were more interested in rolling it as fast as they could.

Karen, Hannie, Nancy, and Margo were taking a different approach. They were rolling the ball very, very slowly. Then they stood at the

110

end of the alley leaning left and right and jumping up and down as if they could influence whether the ball hit anything.

All in all, everybody had their hands full.

Then Claire stomped her foot. "Stop that!" she shouted at her ball, which was just tipping into the gutter. Before anyone could move, she had marched down the bowling alley to try to grab the ball.

"No!" shouted Mal. "Claire!"

But Claire had already bent over and was making slapping motions at the heavy ball, trying to stop it, but afraid it would hurt her somehow. As Mal reached her, Claire straightened up triumphantly and put her foot down on the ball.

Logan, who'd been watching, said, "*Whoa!* If she'd been playing soccer, that would have been a *great* trap."

"Claire," said Mal. "You can't cross over the line. Even if your ball goes in the gutter."

"It's not fair," said Claire. But since she was already holding her bowling ball, she didn't sound too unhappy.

Mal and Claudia kept a close eye on Claire and the other two after that.

Suddenly Linny shouted, "I got a strike! I got a strike!"

Everyone in the bowling alley looked at Linny.

"Good work!" called one of the women who was bowling next to the campers. She grinned and gave Linny a thumbs-up sign.

"I want a strike, too," said Claire.

"If you keep practicing, you might get one," Claudia said diplomatically. But she wasn't hopeful.

Then Jamie jammed all his fingers into the holes of the bowling ball and tried to roll it the way the big kids were doing. Unfortunately, he forgot to take his fingers out when he shoved the ball forward.

In the next second, Jamie was sliding down the bowling lane after his ball.

"Let go!" Claudia shouted. "Jamie, *let go*."

Feeling like a person in a slapstick comedy, she ran after Jamie, who'd slid to a stop, belly down, a few feet down the alley. Just as he stopped, he let go of his ball. It rolled slowly — crept, really — down the alley.

"Jamie, are you okay?" gasped Claudia, trying not to laugh.

Jamie didn't move. He just lay in the lane, his eyes fixed on his snail-moving bowling ball.

Claudia glanced up.

Everyone was looking at them.

"Uh — Jamie," she said.

A huge cheer broke out. Jamie's ball had knocked over all the pins!

What could Claudia do? She helped Jamie to his feet. Jamie clasped his hands over his head and walked proudly back to his seat. Everyone ran to congratulate him.

And Claudia and the rest of the sitters and chaperons spent what was left of the bowling trip trying to convince the other campers that Jamie's method of scoring a strike couldn't be used again.

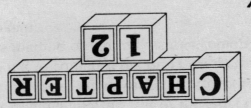

CHAPTER 12

"Y ou sure you don't want to come with us? It's a drive-in movie and it's a really cool, funky old place that they've just reopened," Dawn said.

"I know, I know. You told me. Many times," I said. I was sitting in the den with the remote control for the television in my hand, flipping through the channels.

"It's a double feature," said Sharon. "Two good movies. Really good movies, not junk like last week."

"No, thank you," I said. "My foot hurts."

"You can just stay in the car," Dawn said. "I can get your snacks and stuff."

"No," I said flatly. Then I added reluctantly, "Thanks anyway."

"Maybe another time," said Sharon. "When you're feeling better. . . . Can I get you any-thing before I go?"

"There's juice in the refrigerator," I recited.

"And I can order whatever I want from the take-out places."

"Right," said Sharon after a tiny pause. "Well, see you later, Mary Anne."

" 'Bye," said Dawn.

"Mmm," I said, staring at the television. Not that I was interested in what was on. But I was in the world's meanest, foulest mood. I was in pain (well, I had been for the first couple of days), I was on crutches, and all Sharon and Dawn could think about was partying and being wild and crazy bachelor girls for the last week before my father came back. The night before they'd gone to the county fair and tried to persuade me to limp along with them.

"No," I said. "I don't want people banging into my foot."

I almost hated Sharon and Dawn. And my father.

How would they like it if they'd had a hurt foot and had been abandoned the way I had?

An old dinosaur movie came onto the screen. The dinosaur was stomping along, flattening everything in its path.

I settled back with a sigh. That was *exactly* how I felt.

Meanwhile, the last week of Camp BSC was roaring to a close. The circus act rehearsals were in high gear. Everyone was very, very

excited about the big end-of-camp performance on Friday evening, "real" circus campers and regular campers both.

All the excitement meant that we were extra-
careful to take the kids to the park to play
every morning. It was important for them to
let off some steam before they threw themselves heart and body (literally) into the circus
rehearsals.

I couldn't go to the park. It would have
taken forever for me to hobble over there on
my crutches. And all that crutch-walking
would have made my armpits even more sore
than they already were.

Besides, I had to take care of Alicia, right?
Wrong.

On Wednesday, as the twenty-one campers
divided into buddies and Claire said, "I don't
have a partner," Alicia blurted out, "I'll be
your buddy."

"What?" I exclaimed, before I could stop
myself.

"Great, Alicia," said Claudia casually. "Is
everybody ready, then?"

Of course I knew better than to make a big
deal out of Alicia's sudden decision that it
would be okay to go to the park, that she
didn't have to wait around and make herself
miserable until her mother came to pick her
up.

I didn't say anything except, "Have fun, you guys."

But Alicia stopped and turned anyway. "I was missing all the fun," she said. "Everyone was having a good time without me."

"I'm glad you're going to the park, Alicia. Have a wonderful time."

Alicia smiled. "I will," she said happily, and ran to join Claire and her group.

I stood there and watched the members of Camp BSC disappear down the street.

And tried to think. Something Alicia had said was making a bell go off in my head: everyone was having a good time without me.

Everyone. Sharon and Dawn. Just like Alicia, I'd been missing out on all the fun. I missed my father. But then so did Sharon. And Dawn.

Missing him wasn't going to kill me. But acting like a baby — like a four-year-old — wasn't going to help me, or anyone else either.

What I should have done was make the best of the situation. It might not have helped the time pass faster, or my father come back any sooner, but it certainly would make things easier.

I could hardly wait to tell Mrs. Gianelli about Alicia's giant step forward.

But there was someone else I needed to talk

to, just as soon as Sharon came home from work that day.

"So I'm sorry. I should have talked to you a week and a half ago and told you how I was feeling. Instead I just acted like a baby."

Sharon smiled. "I'm glad you talked to me now, Mary Anne. And I don't think you are being a baby because you miss your father. I miss him, too. Sometimes I feel like having a tantrum and demanding that he come back." She paused and added, "And I expect that he feels the same way sometimes, too. That he wishes he could do something to make us join him instantly."

The idea of Sharon pitching a tantrum, Claire Pike-style, was pretty funny. The idea of my father doing something like that was impossible to imagine.

It made me smile.

"It's nice to see you smile, sweetheart."

"It feels pretty good," I said.

"Well, you've been through a lot these last couple of weeks. And it's true. Dawn and I have been, well, over-indulging in messiness."

"It's not so bad," I said, and I realized that it wasn't really. I mean, it wasn't as if things were going to stay that way. It was more as if the house were on a vacation from being neat.

And that was fine. Things would return to boring old normal soon enough.

Vacations were what made the normal stuff nice. And vice versa.

I leaned over and gave Sharon a hug.

A moment later, Dawn bounced into my room. "Hey, listen to this! You know that drive-in movie? Well, it's changed features and it's got a *new*, totally super double feature playing . . ."

Her voice trailed off. "Do you think you might like to come along, Mary Anne? I mean, I know your leg is hurting and all, but you could sit in the backseat and stretch it out."

"Sound good? It sounds great, in fact," I said. And I realized that it did. I suddenly wanted to laugh. But I didn't. I looked from Sharon to Dawn and said solemnly, "Do you think we can get take-out food delivered to the drive-in?"

CHAPTER 13

If the dress rehearsal is a disaster, that means that the show is going to be a success.

I hoped, by the end of Thursday, that that saying included circuses. Because the Camp BSC circus rehearsal wasn't just a disaster, it was a mega-disaster.

Maybe we should have seen it coming. But with so many kids doing so many different things, we just weren't prepared for the fact that the kids who'd been to the "real" circus camp weren't prepared themselves.

During most of the rehearsals, they'd been standing around watching, not practicing. Even the "real" animal act, involving Carrot, Shannon, Pow, and Noodle had, well, gone to the dogs.

Things started off innocently enough. Kristy had announced the dress rehearsal the day before. So Vanessa came prepared in her ringmaster's costume. She wore white jeans tucked into black rain boots, an old red jacket of her mother's with the sleeves rolled up and a white shirt she'd made with Claudia's help that said *Ringmaster* in sequined script across the chest. She also wore a "top hat" fashioned from painted black cardboard. Vanessa made a great introduction, calling the circus ring a "big top" and only lapsing into poetry occasionally (for instance, when she concluded her speech with, "No matter how things go, I know that you will like our show!").

We all applauded vigorously, and then the first act began. Nicky and Marilyn came out as wild animal trainers. Nicky was carrying a chair and wearing a T-shirt that said *Because I'm the boss, that's why*, and blue sweatpants with a white stripe down the side. Marilyn was wearing blue sweatpants, too. Her T-shirt said *I Brake for Chocolate*. She was carrying a big bag labeled *Treats*.

The wild animals came out and they looked adorable. Claire and Andrew were wearing lion manes made of felt and yarn. Andrew wore a T-shirt painted orange and black with an orange and black striped face. They roared and meowed like cats and switched their tails and stroked their painted-on cat whiskers and furry ears attached to headbands. And if Alicia didn't look exactly like a camel, she still made a very impressive wild animal.

The animal trainers put the wild animals through their paces with only minimal mishaps: Claire tripped as she jumped through a hoop of fire (a hula hoop with red, orange, and yellow crepe paper glued to it) and Andrew crashed into her from behind. They recovered nicely and roared at each other until Nicky approached them with the chair and commanded them to go back to their places. They returned to their perches (bales of hay with colorful old tablecloths on top) and roared some more. Meanwhile Jamie pretended to do a tiger dance on his hind legs and Alicia jumped over some special hurdles.

We all applauded, and Nicky and Marilyn bowed, and Marilyn handed treats to the wild animals.

Then the animal dancers came on and the disaster began. Jessi had choreographed a simple dance that incorporated things that the kids could already do (such as Margo's terrific cartwheels and Becca's ability to walk on her hands). And clearly Becca, who'd chosen to be a goat (after her rhino head didn't quite work) and Margo, who'd chosen to be a bird, had practiced their parts. But Ricky and Hannie didn't seem to know what they were doing at all. When Ricky lost his place in the animal dance line for the fifth time, he scowled and said, "Well, animals don't dance in real circuses, either," and stopped altogether. Hannie stopped, too, which left Becca and Margo spinning in a void.

Then Becca and Margo stopped. "We're all supposed to be touching our right hands together in the center and turning around in an animal wheel," said Becca.

"No real animal in a real circus would ever do that."

"This is *our* circus," Margo said indignantly. "We can do what we want."

"It's dumb," said Ricky.

"Oh, yeah?" Margo put her hands on her hips and looked very threatening (at least, very threatening for a bird).

"Curtain, curtain, curtain!" said Vanessa. She jumped to the middle of the ring.

"Don't you know any of the steps?" asked Becca, her voice sounding a little wobbly. "Jessi made this dance up for four animals. We can't do it with only two!"

"Curtain," said Vanessa. *"Bring on the clowns."* Kristy dropped a new cassette into the tape deck and the clowns — David Michael, Matt, Carolyn, and Natalie — came tumbling into the ring, waving squirt guns and wearing big red noses made of Ping-Pong balls, and funny faces that they'd painted on themselves — all except Natalie.

"Natalie, where's your costume?" asked Kristy, stopping the music with a slam of her hand. Her voice echoed loudly in the silence.

Natalie said, "It didn't look like a real clown costume. So I just never finished it."

"Our costumes look *real*," said David Michael. "Our costumes look great!"

"Natalie, go stand over there with Mary Anne. We'll talk about the costume later."

The clowns went on with the show.

"The water's making the clowns' makeup run," said Natalie loudly. "That's because it's not real clown makeup."

David Michael ran toward the audience with what looked like a big bucket of water. He threw the bucket — on Natalie.

Natalie gave a little scream before she realized that the bucket was filled with oatmeal.

"That's a real clown trick," said David Michael angrily.

"Clowns, stay in character. I mean, keep on being funny, not angry, okay?" Kristy called out.

The clowns finished their act — with more than one furious look in Natalie's direction.

"And now for our specialty acts, beginning with sawing the lady in half," said Vanessa.

This was the secret act that Karen and Nancy had been working on.

"This would be better if we were a real circus camp with real props," Karen announced in her biggest, loudest "outdoor" voice. "But we had to make our own. We hope the audience will understand."

"Hey, I'm supposed to make the announcements," said Vanessa, brandishing her baton. "I'm the ringmaster."

"Then why are you holding a baton?" said Karen scornfully. "You look like a bandleader in a parade, not a real ringmaster."

Vanessa's eyes flashed. But she was never at a loss for words and this time proved no exception. "Cut it out, you two! Or you will soon be *through!*"

Karen rolled her eyes. Then she motioned to Nancy to crawl into a big cardboard box that said *Under the counter storage system* on one side and *This side up* on the other. They'd put the box on the bale of hay and cut a door in the top, which Karen ceremoniously raised for Nancy to climb through. There was a hole in one end of the box for Nancy's head and two holes at the other end for her feet. After a moment of thumping and bumping, Nancy's head popped out of one end. A moment later, a strange and lumpy looking "leg" emerged from the other end. Then another "leg" emerged.

Beside me, Logan started to snicker. "What is that?"

I peered at the "legs." "They look like stockings stuffed with . . . toilet paper?"

"I will now saw Nancy in half. Nancy, please wiggle your legs to demonstrate that is really you in the box."

The two lumpy legs wiggled. Oddly.

Karen produced a small saw and held it high in the air.

Every single sitter there jumped forward at once, saying, "Stop! Hold it right there! What are you doing?"

Karen stopped, looking surprised and a little sheepish.

"Where did you get that saw?" demanded Kristy, who had reached Karen first.

"F-from the barn." Seeing my friends and me converge on her at once had shaken Karen's confidence.

"And what were you going to do with it?"

"Pretend to saw people in half. Kristy! This is a real saw because you need real things if you are going to have a real circus!"

"Karen." Kristy ran her hands through her hair so it stood up every which way. "I'm glad you and your friends went to circus camp. But that doesn't mean you know everything about circuses. And let me tell you, a little bit of knowledge is a dangerous thing."

Karen frowned.

Kristy frowned.

I said, "Everyone who was at the circus camp learned things. But true performers always do what they are supposed to do. And you guys haven't done that. Now it looks like the circus might not go on."

Karen's eyes grew huge behind her glasses. Nancy sniffed. Then she wriggled, trying to get out of the box — and one of the stuffed legs fell off!

Well, that did it. The tension was broken. We all started laughing.

At least all us sitters did. The kids were silent. Awesomely silent.

Then Karen said in a small voice, "I'm sorry."

"I'm sorry, too," Nancy wailed. "Get me out of here."

"What are we going to do?" Vanessa asked.

"We keep practicing," said Kristy. "We run through the show and then we see what we can do to fix it up. Karen, we'll talk later."

Things didn't exactly improve after that. The high-board act that Bobby and Chris performed didn't involve any real saws. It also didn't involve any interesting tricks. Clearly, Bobby and Chris hadn't been practicing either.

And the dog show was almost a real dog.

Hannie and Linny had tried to teach Noodle a whole bunch of new tricks. As a result, Noodle was thoroughly confused. Whenever they said anything, he looked around. Most of the time he just sat. Or raised his paw to shake hands.

"A real circus dog," Linny began to say in frustration, then stopped himself and looked around, " . . . um, takes a long, long time to train, I guess."

"I guess," said Vanessa.

"Carrot can still say his prayers," said Charlotte.

"Shannon speaks when you tell her to," said David Michael.

"Pow will lie down on his side when you tell him to nap," said Margo.

"Noodle will go fetch whatever you point to," volunteered Hannie. "That's his best trick."

"What are we going to do?" asked Vanessa again.

"We're going to re-edit our show," said Dawn. "We'll start from the beginning. But everybody has to cooperate."

129

"We've got a lot of work to do between now and tomorrow," Shannon said.

"Emergency meeting of the BSC," added Kristy. "Right over here." She pointed to one side of the ring.

"Okay, you guys, get your buddy from this morning and go sit over there." Logan pointed to the other side of the ring.

It was an amazing thing to ask twenty-two kids ages four to nine to do. But they did it. Lions and a tiger and an elephant and a goat and a camel and all the others sat down and waited while we had a quick emergency meeting of the BSC.

"What *are* we going to do?" hissed Kristy as we huddled together. Dawn and I ex-changed glances. Wow. Kristy almost never asks that question. She usually has at least an opinion about what people should do.

Mal said thoughtfully, "I think I have an idea for the dog act. A sort of plot . . ."

Jessi said, "We can rework the dance so that all Ricky and Hannie do is more or less stand still."

"With a cardboard saw, Karen might be able to pull off a pretty funny act," I said. Kristy was beginning to look more cheerful. We all were.

Logan said, "Why don't we use the high-board act as part of the clown act? I think I see a way we can do it. And a way we can include all the clowns."

"We can do it," Dawn said.

"No problem," agreed Claudia.

"Okay, great." Kristy turned briskly. "Let's get to work. The show must and *will* go on!"

CHAPTER 14

The show did go on.

On Friday morning, the moment the last parent had dropped off the last camper, Camp BSC went into fast forward.

I put Karen and Nancy to work making a cardboard saw. We all put last-minute touches on costumes. Jessi led the dancers through a revised version of the wild animal dance. Logan, Chris, and Bobby made many trips to and from the barn to where the high-board act was set up. Meanwhile, laughter and Pow's unmistakable baying came from the rehearsal of the four dogs and their trainers.

At midmorning we took a break for our last trip together to the park. The dogs went along this time, but I couldn't go. Alicia left happily, without a backward glance, and I actually thought, "Wow, they grow up *so* fast." I caught myself and had to laugh.

There was plenty for me to do at home while

Camp BSC was at the park. I made extra batches of circus punch (fruit juice and ginger ale and chunks of fruit cut into funny shapes) for the campers to have with their last lunch at Camp BSC. And I made sure enough candy apples were ready for a surprise dessert.

I'd just finished getting organized when the campers returned. They were no longer divided into the SMS and the SES factions. They were all rambling along together. And they were singing.

When I heard what they were singing I burst out laughing. Apparently the official song of Camp BSC had become any song with the word "bowling" stuck in at strategic places.

After lunch and quiet time (spent reassuring Vanessa that she was going to be a terrific ringmaster and promising Bobby and Chris that we would be *right* there if anything went wrong) we began to make the final preparations for the Camp BSC Circus. Together we popped up the popcorn, arranged the folding chairs and picnic table benches, and of course sampled plenty of the food to make sure that it tasted just right for the customers.

Then the parents began to arrive. And the grandparents. And the sisters and brothers and friends. Half a dozen adults brought video cameras, including Mr. Ramsey, who promised the members of the BSC copies of their very own.

"I know you'll want to have it to remember this by," he said, panning the crowd with his camera. "Looks like it's going to be a great circus!"

I said, "Thanks, Mr. Ramsey. That'll be super." My eyes met Logan's. "And you're right. It's going to be a great circus."

Vanessa put her fingers in her mouth and whistled loudly. It was a skill none of us had realized she had. It got our attention. And the crowd's.

I felt a hand on my shoulder. "So you're in charge of the refreshments?"

"Sharon! You got off work early!" I exclaimed.

"I wouldn't have missed this for the world. You and Dawn have been working so hard."

"Dawn's in the barn with the performers, helping them get ready," I said. "I'm so glad you came."

"Me, too." Sharon gave my shoulder another squeeze — and Vanessa gave another piercing whistle.

With an elaborate clearing of her throat, Vanessa said, "Ladies and gentlemen . . ."

Needless to say, the wild animal act was a *huge* success, especially when the animals jumped through the hoop of "fire." And when Alicia stopped in mid-trick to turn and wave at her parents, it brought the house down.

The animal dancers were next, and I admit that I held my breath. I think Jessi was a little bit nervous, too. And Ricky and Hannie were concentrating so intensely that they forgot to smile when they walked into the center of the ring.

But when the dance began and things went smoothly, they relaxed. Margo's cartwheels earned applause, as did Becca's walking on her hands. And it was amazing. Whatever Jessi had done, the four of them looked as if they knew exactly what they were doing and had practiced it a million times. It was only if you knew what had gone on that you realized Ricky and Hannie were doing a lot of spinning in place and cross-the-ring swoops.

By the end of the dance, all the wild animals were smiling and they took their bows to cries of "Bravo" from the audience.

The clowns came tumbling out next and, thanks to Claudia and Shannon and Dawn's hard work, Natalie's clown costume was just as goofy as the others. The kids had (with the help of Claud's keen artistic eye) painted on great clown faces. They chased each other and "tripped" over their big feet and brandished squirt guns and pillows and had a great time. When they were done, they were completely out of breath, covered in water (and a little oatmeal), and laughing as hard as the audience. They took their bows in classic clown form: Whenever one of them bent over, another would pretend to kick him in the rear, and send him sprawling.

And the specialty acts? Well, Nancy's "leg" fell off again the moment Karen started sawing, and the crowd burst into laugher and applause. Karen's face grew very red, but when she realized that the crowd enjoyed it, she turned into an old stage performer before our eyes. She picked up the leg and stuck it back in the hole in the box — upside down.

Karen sawed the box in half with her cardboard saw. (The box was really two boxes joined together, with Nancy scrunched up in one box with her head sticking out of the side.)

The crowd applauded and Karen bowed. Nancy jumped up and poked her legs through the bottom of her box and took a bow, too. Well pleased with the roar of approval, the two girls took a final bow and left the ring for the high-board act.

It had definitely improved. I'm not sure what Logan had done, but the high-board act had become a clown act all on its own, with Bobby pretending to be afraid to climb all the way up and Chris trying to persuade him. It ended with both boys on the board, doing silly, crazy, tricks, and falling off in the end into a big pile of hay.

Then Vanessa announced the final act: Dr. Dog.

"Oh dear, oh dear," said Hannie. "Something is wrong with poor Pow!"

"Yes!" said Margo. "All Pow will do all day long is NAP, POW."

Pow looked at Margo. "That's what he does, don't you, Pow. You just NAP."

Slowly Pow sat down and then slid his front paws out. He rolled over on his side and lay still.

"Oh dear, oh dear, what should we do?" said Margo.

David Michael said, "We must send for Dr. Dog!"

"But he is so far away!"

"Don't worry," said Hannie. "We can send brave Noodle and Shannon to FETCH him. She bent toward Noodle and pointed to Linny and Charlotte, who were waiting at the other end of the ring with Carrot.

"FETCH Dr. Dog and LINNY, Noodle. Shannon, go."

Noodle got up and started to trot to Linny. Shannon stayed where she'd been told to sit at the beginning of the show, her tongue hanging out, looking cheerfully around at the audience.

"I will go, too!" David Michael cried. He ran to Noodle. Over his shoulder he said, "Here, Shannon!"

Shannon jumped up instantly and raced after David Michael.

When they reached Charlotte and Linny, David Michael told Shannon to sit. (Noodle was already sitting).

"What do you want?" asked Charlotte. "Would you like to SPEAK, SHANNON to Dr. Dog about something?"

Shannon wagged her tail.

"Yes, Shannon, SPEAK to Dr. Dog."

You could almost see a little light go off in Shannon's brain. "Arf!" she said happily. "Arf, arf."

"That sick, huh?" said Charlotte. "We'd better get going, Dr. Dog."

The doctor hurried back to the patient. Charlotte sat down on a bale of hay next to Pow (who had begun to wag *his* tail).

"Dr. Dog must think," announced Charlotte. She leaned over and whispered, "Say your prayers, Carrot." Carrot put his paws in Charlotte's lap and lowered his head.

"Good boy," Charlotte whispered loudly.

Carrot took his paws down and barked loudly.

"Look, Pow is getting UP, POW. He's cured," cried Hannie.

Pow jumped up.

And the audience broke into the loudest applause yet. Of course the dogs all barked and jumped around.

Mal, I thought, you are a *genius*.

Everyone came running out from the barn then, and the parents gave them three ovations. Then people milled around, eating and drinking and talking. They seemed reluctant to leave and it was almost dark before the last group of parents and kids drifted toward their cars. Most of the kids had asked if we could do it again.

Best of all was Alicia, who let go of her mother's hand to come tearing back to me. She threw her arms around my legs (crutches and all). " 'Bye, Mary Anne," she said. "Camp was the funnest thing I ever did. Can we have camp again?"

"Next year, Alicia," I promised. "Next year!"

CHAPTER 15

I woke up the morning after the circus feeling cheerful and contented and generally pleased with the world. And not just because Camp BSC had been such a success.

There was another reason: we were going to pick my father up from the airport that afternoon.

And we were going to spend the morning making it look like the wild and crazy bachelor girls were the neatniks of the earth.

Okay, so housework doesn't make me cheerful. Who does like doing it? But I enjoyed the morning with Dawn and Sharon. We sang and goofed and told jokes — and mopped and swept and did a gazillion loads of dishes and laundry and everything else. Even with a sprained ankle, you can get quite a lot done!

By the time we left for the airport, our house was spotless.

We made Dad a big bouquet of flowers from

the garden. And we all flung ourselves at him when he came through the door into the waiting area at the airport.

"How are my girls doing?" he said, laughing and hugging us hard.

"Great," I said, and I meant it.

That night, after dinner, I had a long talk with Dad, though. I told him what had happened and how much I had missed him. "It really kind of surprised me, Dad," I said. "I mean, I'm practically grown up, but . . ."

My father nodded thoughtfully.

"Do you have to travel?" I asked. "Do you have to stay away so long?"

"Well, yes, I do."

"Oh." My heart sank. I almost wanted to cry. Don't be silly, I told myself. Your dad is here now. Worry about him being away when the time comes.

My father hadn't finished yet, however. "Maybe, though, I can arrange to travel less. Or make shorter trips. And things will settle down once the details of this merger have been sorted out."

"Oh," I said again, feeling a little more cheerful. It wasn't exactly the solution I would have chosen. But it sounded better than nothing.

"You have to promise me something, though," said my father.

"Sure. What?"

And then my dad, Mr. Neat and Organized, said something I never thought I'd hear him say. "Loosen up a little," he told me. "Enjoy yourself. I know you love Sharon, but I think you might feel even closer to her if you let yourself have some fun. And try to talk to her. Don't let your feelings pile up like, like dirty dishes."

I burst out laughing. "You've got a promise!"

"Hey, guys," Sharon stuck her head into my bedroom. "What about that video?"

Jessi and Mal had biked by that afternoon while we were at the airport and left a copy of the Camp BSC Circus Video.

"Come on, Dad," I said, jumping up. "We're about to show you a truly excellent video. Academy Award stuff at least. But if you *don't* think so," I looked at Sharon, "well, we can show you how to express yourself with popcorn!"

Laughing, we went to join Dawn.

"A quiet time for the BSC," said Kristy, sitting in her director's chair in Claudia's room. We were passing around junk food and talking. Logan wasn't there — he was playing baseball at the park — but the rest of the Camp BSC counselors were sitting around the room, eating junk food and waiting for the phone to ring. It was almost six and, so far, we had taken only two calls.

"Lots of kids are away at overnight camp," said Jessi. "The Braddocks, Natalie."

"The Giannellis have gone on vacation," I said. "But when they get back, the kids are going to be doing stuff at the community center. Mrs. Giannelli called to tell me that Alicia is looking forward to it. She wants to know if will be like the circus she was in this summer."

"Speaking of circuses, Karen and Hannie and Nancy are already working on their circus act for next summer," Kristy said. "And Hannie and Linny are taking tumbling classes at the community center because they think they can use it in the next Camp BSC circus!"

"So I guess we're a real circus camp after all," Claudia said.

"Well, I'm glad the BSC has hit a lull. My family is about to do its summer vacation trip to the shore," announced Shannon. "So I won't be here next week or the week after."

"The beach." Dawn looked envious.

"I'd love to go to the beach, too," Mal said. "Even if I do get sunburned. But I think we're going on a camping trip." She wrinkled her nose. There was a moment of silence as we imagined the havoc the Pikes could wreak on a camping trip.

Claudia cleared her throat. "Uh, good luck, Mal."

Mal grinned.

"What about you?" Jessi teased me. "You and Logan. Any big summer plans, once you are off your crutches?"

I thought for a moment. Then I shook my head. "I'm going to take it easy," I said. "Hang out with my family. Enjoy having my dad home again." I looked around the room. "That's what summer's for, you know. Sometimes, the best vacation of all is just learning to loosen up!"

About the Author

ANN M. MARTIN did *a lot* of baby-sitting when she was growing up in Princeton, New Jersey. She is a former editor of books for children, and was graduated from Smith College.

Ms. Martin lives in New York City with her cats, Mouse and Rosie. She likes ice cream and *I Love Lucy*; and she hates to cook.

Ann Martin's Apple Paperbacks include *Yours Turly, Shirley*; *Ten Kids, No Pets*; *With You and Without You*; *Bummer Summer*; and all the other books in the Baby-sitters Club series.

About the Author

WILLIAM M. JASPERSOHN is an award-winning author who lives near Boston. A former teacher and magazine editor, he has written more than a dozen books for children and young adults, including *How the Forest Grew*, *A Week in the Life of a Firefighter*, *The Ballpark: One Day Behind the Scenes at a Major League Game*, and others.

THE BABY-SITTERS CLUB

Look for #87
STACEY AND THE BAD GIRLS

Once, during a school work project at the mall, I discovered just how common shoplifting is. I knew that store managers often keep their eyes on suspicious-acting people and gangs of teens.

When I turned back around, my friends were gone.

"Sheil?" I called out. "Mia?"

I looked up the next aisle, but they weren't there. I walked around a large wall display of sportswear, and into book department.

The four of them were in the thrillers section. I spotted Sheila looking at a paperback, then giving it to Heather. "Hey, guys!" I called out.

Sheila spun around. "Oh. Hi."

"What are you reading?" I asked. But when I was close enough to see Heather, she had nothing in her hand.

"I don't know, just some horror book," Heather replied. "Sheila likes them, not me."

"Oh," I said.

"Can we go now?" Mia asked.

Jacqui was already heading for the door. Sheila, Mia, and I followed her.

Behind us, I could hear the click of Heather's shoulder bag buckle.

My stomach began to sink. I imagined Heather taking away the book inside her bag. Stealing it.

Nahh, no way. I was just being oversensitive.

Then I thought about the time Logan Bruno started hanging out with a bunch of tough guys who liked to shoplift. They brought nice, innocent Logan with them on purpose, because shopowners wouldn't suspect them as much. In other words, they used him (the creeps).

Was that happening with me?

Read all the books
about **Mary Anne**
in the Baby-sitters Club series
by Ann M. Martin

4 *Mary Anne Saves the Day*
Mary Anne is tired of being treated like a baby.
It's time to take charge!

#10 *Logan Likes Mary Anne!*
Mary Anne has a crush on a *boy* baby-sitter!

#17 *Mary Anne's Bad-Luck Mystery*
Will Mary Anne's bad luck ever go away?

#25 *Mary Anne and the Search for Tigger*
Tigger is missing! Has he been cat-napped?

#30 *Mary Anne and the Great Romance*
Mary Anne's father and Dawn's mother are getting
married!

#34 *Mary Anne and Too Many Boys*
Will a summer romance come between Mary Anne
and Logan?

#41 *Mary Anne vs. Logan*
Mary Anne thought she and Logan would be together forever. . . .

#46 *Mary Anne Misses Logan*
But does Logan miss *her*?

#52 *Mary Anne + 2 Many Babies*
Whoever thought taking care of a bunch of babies could be so much trouble?

#60 *Mary Anne's Makeover*
Everyone loves the new Mary Anne — *except* the BSC!

#66 *Maid Mary Anne*
Mary Anne's a baby-sitter — not a housekeeper!

#73 *Mary Anne and Miss Priss*
What will Mary Anne do with a kid who is *too* perfect?

#79 *Mary Anne Breaks the Rules*
Boyfriends and baby-sitting don't always mix.

#86 *Mary Anne and Camp BSC*
Mary Anne is in for loads of summer fun!

Mysteries:

 # 5 *Mary Anne and the Secret in the Attic*
Mary Anne discovers a secret about her past and now she's afraid of the future!

#13 *Mary Anne and the Library Mystery*
There's a Readathon going on and someone's setting fires in the Stoneybrook library!

#20 *Mary Anne and the Zoo Mystery*
Someone is freeing the animals at the Bedford Zoo!

THE BABY-SITTERS CLUB®

by Ann M. Martin

☐ MG43388-1	#1	Kristy's Great Idea	$3.50
☐ MG43387-3	#10	Logan Likes Mary Anne!	$3.50
☐ MG43717-8	#15	Little Miss Stoneybrook...and Dawn	$3.50
☐ MG43722-4	#20	Kristy and the Walking Disaster	$3.50
☐ MG43347-4	#25	Mary Anne and the Search for Tigger	$3.50
☐ MG42498-X	#30	Mary Anne and the Great Romance	$3.50
☐ MG42497-1	#31	Dawn's Wicked Stepsister	$3.50
☐ MG42496-3	#32	Kristy and the Secret of Susan	$3.50
☐ MG42495-5	#33	Claudia and the Great Search	$3.25
☐ MG42494-7	#34	Mary Anne and Too Many Boys	$3.50
☐ MG42508-0	#35	Stacey and the Mystery of Stoneybrook	$3.50
☐ MG43565-5	#36	Jessi's Baby-sitter	$3.50
☐ MG43566-3	#37	Dawn and the Older Boy	$3.25
☐ MG43567-1	#38	Kristy's Mystery Admirer	$3.25
☐ MG43568-X	#39	Poor Mallory!	$3.25
☐ MG44082-9	#40	Claudia and the Middle School Mystery	$3.25
☐ MG43570-1	#41	Mary Anne Versus Logan	$3.50
☐ MG44083-7	#42	Jessi and the Dance School Phantom	$3.50
☐ MG43572-8	#43	Stacey's Emergency	$3.50
☐ MG43573-6	#44	Dawn and the Big Sleepover	$3.50
☐ MG43574-4	#45	Kristy and the Baby Parade	$3.50
☐ MG43569-8	#46	Mary Anne Misses Logan	$3.50
☐ MG44971-0	#47	Mallory on Strike	$3.50
☐ MG43571-X	#48	Jessi's Wish	$3.50
☐ MG44970-2	#49	Claudia and the Genius of Elm Street	$3.25
☐ MG44969-9	#50	Dawn's Big Date	$3.50
☐ MG44968-0	#51	Stacey's Ex-Best Friend	$3.50
☐ MG44966-4	#52	Mary Anne + 2 Many Babies	$3.50
☐ MG44967-2	#53	Kristy for President	$3.25
☐ MG44965-6	#54	Mallory and the Dream Horse	$3.25
☐ MG44964-8	#55	Jessi's Gold Medal	$3.25
☐ MG45657-1	#56	Keep Out, Claudia!	$3.50
☐ MG45658-X	#57	Dawn Saves the Planet	$3.50

More titles... ▶

☐ MG45659-8	#58 Stacey's Choice	$3.50
☐ MG45660-1	#59 Mallory Hates Boys (and Gym)	$3.50
☐ MG45662-8	#60 Mary Anne's Makeover	$3.50
☐ MG45663-6	#61 Jessi's and the Awful Secret	$3.50
☐ MG45664-4	#62 Kristy and the Worst Kid Ever	$3.50
☐ MG45665-2	#63 Claudia's ~~Freind~~ Friend	$3.50
☐ MG45666-0	#64 Dawn's Family Feud	$3.50
☐ MG45667-9	#65 Stacey's Big Crush	$3.50
☐ MG47004-3	#66 Maid Mary Anne	$3.50
☐ MG47005-1	#67 Dawn's Big Move	$3.50
☐ MG47006-X	#68 Jessi and the Bad Baby-Sitter	$3.50
☐ MG47007-8	#69 Get Well Soon, Mallory!	$3.50
☐ MG47008-6	#70 Stacey and the Cheerleaders	$3.50
☐ MG47009-4	#71 Claudia and the Perfect Boy	$3.50
☐ MG47010-8	#72 Dawn and the We Love Kids Club	$3.50
☐ MG45575-3	Logan's Story Special Edition Readers' Request	$3.25
☐ MG47118-X	Logan Bruno, Boy Baby-sitter Special Edition Readers' Request	$3.50
☐ MG44240-6	Baby-sitters on Board! Super Special #1	$3.95
☐ MG44239-2	Baby-sitters' Summer Vacation Super Special #2	$3.95
☐ MG43973-1	Baby-sitters' Winter Vacation Super Special #3	$3.95
☐ MG42493-9	Baby-sitters' Island Adventure Super Special #4	$3.95
☐ MG43575-2	California Girls! Super Special #5	$3.95
☐ MG43576-0	New York, New York! Super Special #6	$3.95
☐ MG44963-X	Snowbound Super Special #7	$3.95
☐ MG44962-X	Baby-sitters at Shadow Lake Super Special #8	$3.95
☐ MG45661-X	Starring the Baby-sitters Club Super Special #9	$3.95
☐ MG45674-1	Sea City, Here We Come! Super Special #10	$3.95

Available wherever you buy books...or use this order form.

Scholastic Inc., P.O. Box 7502, 2931 E. McCarty Street, Jefferson City, MO 65102

Please send me the books I have checked above. I am enclosing $_____
(please add $2.00 to cover shipping and handling). Send check or money order - no
cash or C.O.D.s please.

Name _____ Birthdate_____

Address _____

City_____ State/Zip _____
Please allow four to six weeks for delivery. Offer good in the U.S. only. Sorry, mail orders are not
available to residents of Canada. Prices subject to change.

BSC993